To Pan my
friend.
Hope you enjoy my
efforts

WHO KILLED THE
RAGGY MEN?

Cheers!

Alan M. Etheridge

A. Etheridge

March 2024

CW01376266

 New Generation Publishing

ACKNOWLEDGEMENTS

As ever, without the encouragement of my wife Valerie, this book would never have been written. I must also thank her for her assistance with the artwork necessary for the design of the book's cover. I also thank Tim Plumb for his work in proofreading.

DEDICATION

I dedicate this book to the memory of my brother-in-law, Bill, a man who brought much happiness into our lives.

The Green Man.

In a lonely grave The Green Man lay,
And sleeps by night and sleeps by day.
But the King is dead, Tom King is dead,
So place the mask upon his head.
And soon he'll be in sacred earth,
How false the tears, how oft the mirth?

Prologue

Legend had it that the terrifying storm that brought the great yew tree crashing to the ground, ending more than a thousand years of history was no chance happening. Channelling the brook entailed making a cutting through the churchyard on into the mainstream before draining into the River Severn.

Church records were meticulously scanned and none of the ancient graves in that long since abandoned area would be disturbed. The dead would stay locked in a dreamless sleep in the earth below. Crumbling, lichen-stained local sandstone recorded that the last tenant was a certain: 'Gabriel Longstreet. Yeoman of this parish and the finest ploughman in the county. He served his earthly master well and now doth serve our Master in Heaven. RIP year of our Lord 1759.' No mere country man could have afforded such a monument. This was a long dead landowner showing his gratitude to an honest and hard-working man of the land.

In an age when the face of Britain was experiencing rapid change and canals were networking the land, no piece of earth deemed valuable for wealth production could be left fallow. Thus, the channelling of water to convert bogs into fertile grazing land was a mission to be speedily undertaken. The population was growing; the population required feeding. Every extra acre meant increased wealth for the owners.

Navvies previously employed on canals were in plentiful supply. Frugal income might be spent on ale or in local whorehouses, leaving little for food. When the workers were unfit to work, monies were subtracted from their wages and meal tokens were issued and exchanged for a bowl of soup and a portion of bread. These were hard men whose lives depended upon pick and shovel, but also men who still believed in the Devil and all his works.

The work at Upper Egginton was proceeding apace until the storm. Although the weather had been oppressive, men laboured from dawn till dusk, sweat streaking in rivulets down their muscular earth-stained bodies. All knew that a storm was brewing, none knew when. When it came, the deluge filled cuttings, caused earth slides and put back the work done by some weeks.

Then it was over, with clear blue skies and fresh winds carrying the metallic smell associated with the cleansing rain. Labourers working in the tarn were offered a little extra to clear away the fallen yew tree and fill in the huge crater left by its root formation. Work progressed steadily. Once the yew had been dragged to the side using man and shire-horse power, the gang divided into two groups; one armed with two-handled saws, the other bringing barrow loads of soil plundered from previous workings. Men swore and beasts slid in the ever-deepening mud surrounding the tree.

As with the bolt of lightning which had destroyed the ancient conifer, it happened suddenly and totally without warning.

"Jesus, Mary and Joseph!" exclaimed the heavily accented Irish voice.

"Will yer just look at this?"

The burley foreman had thrown down his pick and was pointing into the fissure. Some six feet below, the rictus grin of a masklike skull gazed up at the horrified men. Its teeth still gleamed. The eye sockets were stark and black. These men had seen skeletal remains many times in their excavations but this skull was so terrible to look upon that many turned and ran. Devout Catholics amongst the crew crossed themselves. A fine flimsy filament of roots covered the face giving the impression of a lacy veil. The major root formations had penetrated every orifice giving the appearance of hair both as skull cap and beard. The cry went up amongst the assembled navvies:

"The Green Man! The Green Man! Tis Jack in the Green."

A lone voice shouted;

"Fetch the priest!"

Chapter 1

Stars illuminated the dark night sky. The cooling warmth of the previous day still carried subtle wafts of apple blossom from the ancient orchards of gnarled, lichen-encrusted trees in nearby gardens. Bella King was fast asleep after a hard day in the bar.

The black BMW had been taken to the car wash during the day and in the buttery light from the street lamp, it gleamed as if in showroom condition. Tom King enjoyed the luxury of the cream leather interior and that feeling that he could out speed most cars should he so wish. Many villagers would have gladly 'keyed' the vehicle had there been the possibility of doing this without The Green Man's guvnor being aware. None had so far plucked up the courage to attempt what many would have delighted in.

He gently drew his hand along the length of the vehicle and felt an almost sensual thrill. It was then that his gaze fell upon what appeared to be some kind of note or envelope pressed under a windscreen wiper. Under his breath he muttered,

"What the f'ing hell is this? Some bloody advert for dry-cleaning or buy one get one free from the local pizza parlour? If the wiper's damaged I'll make 'em pay!"

Tom King snatched the offending envelope from the windscreen and ripped it open. A small folded note dropped out onto the pavement. He stooped, picked it up and held it up to the light. Letters, cut it would seem from a newspaper had been glued onto a blank piece of crumpled paper. As he had unfolded the paper, a letter obviously not securely affixed floated lazily to the ground. The message was never the less unequivocal: 'YOU BASTARD! I KNOW WHAT YOU DID AND YOU'LL PAY.OH ES YOU'LL PAY!' The 'Y' lay on the ground for a moment before a gentle breeze caught it up in its swirl and whisked it away. King pondered the message for a moment, smiled, screwed it into a ball and aimed it at the lamp's column.

"You can try mate!"

King shrugged and pressed a button on his car key pad before opening the driver's side door. He smoothed down his already immaculate suit, flicked away a torn piece of white paper from the letter and sniffed at the bunch of red roses in his hand before placing them carefully on the back seat. The bottle of Prosecco which he had retrieved from the cooling cabinet in the pub lay beside him on the passenger seat. This was going to be an easy and cheap night out. A bottle of cheap plonk and a bunch of flowers was all it cost for what he anticipated would be a satisfying steamy bedroom romp.

Chapter 2

Jim Walsh aka 'Whitsun Willy' was not a happy Morris dancer.

"Bugger, sod it, shit!"

He mumbled as he fought off the temptation to do a Basil Fawlty by kicking rather than whipping the car. Today of all days, he thought. Well, I'll just have to phone Jakey and risk looking a prize prat. Jakey, aka Round Jake, was a mechanic of some repute; tattooed in deep blue from head to toe, weighing twenty stone plus and reeking of Brut Aftershave and axel grease. Jakey had used Brut since the Seventies as a teenager and was known to quote the advertisement featuring Henry Cooper. His mock cockney retort to anyone daring to suggest that perhaps he might change his signature scent was always.

"The great smell of Brut. Just slap it on."

Jake was capable of divesting himself of his overalls, donning his 'Raggy Man' outfit and dancing like an overweight fawn. Yes, Round Jakey was a Raggy Man through and through. When asked an opinion about a second-hand car that one of his dance troupe was contemplating purchasing, Jake did much more than kick the tyres and give a 'Yes' or 'No'. If you asked for his advice, he'd place the vehicle under the Jakey microscope and give details. Jakey was to cars what the hospital consultant was to illness. With him, you would get a full diagnosis and even a health check and forecast as to when a vehicle might no longer be viable.

On being asked for an opinion regarding Jim's planned purchase of a ten-year-old Escort, he needed little time to make his pronouncement:

"It's a nail, Jim. Wouldn't touch it with a disinfected bargepole."

Even so, Jim had argued that from a financial standpoint at a mere four hundred pounds, it was worth a punt.

"Be it on yer own bloody 'ead Jim. It might cost yer four hundred quid now but I'll guarantee you'll be spending more than that within six months on repairs. The clutch is knackered, there's rust everywhere and I wouldn't pass it for its next MOT."

Jim now ruefully admitted that Jakey had been absolutely correct in his forecast. The car had proved to be a money pit and even with his friend's special rates, he was a further seven hundred pounds out of pocket and problems were still arising. Now here he was on a beautiful May morning, a car full of Raggy gear and in need of some means of transportation to The Green Man pub ready for the afternoon festivities.

To Jim, Morris dancing was not just a bit of fun and an excuse for a jig around and crashing sticks before a beery booze-up. Morris was his life. He had formed the Raggy Men team and trained them with almost military precision. Prior to his move to Bridgnorth, he had been a dancer down in the Cotswolds. Jim was a Morris Dance 'anorak'. Each area had its own traditions and he favoured handkerchiefs and sticks. He needed six or eight men for the group dances and a couple who could perform solo or dual. Some traditions used flexible spring steel swords, some wooden swords; some waved flags rather than handkerchiefs. Other groups still blacked up in spite of the being hounded by the various pressure groups. There were many such groups who might take a day off from demonstrating against foxhunting or whatever happened to be the current cause celebre to wave their banners and claim that the dancers were racist. Recently there had been an anti-Morris rally directed at a local group whose style was known as Border Morris. The Bunford Bedlams group had blacked up as was required by tradition supposedly to hide the identity of the dancers. Things had got nasty as locals and dancers alike faced down strangers from other parts of the country. The local police became involved. Jim was careful to avoid such embarrassments. Jim Walsh was a strictly law-abiding citizen with an embedded respect for the police and the judiciary.

For Jim, it would always be 'Cotswold' although he had been forced to make concessions in some areas of the dancing. His advertisement in the post office in Bridgnorth had to his delight been answered by more than enough potential dancing men. He had interviewed them before whittling down the numbers. He had chosen men with qualifications that included: dancing ability; youth and most importantly, bushy beards. This latter was necessary to enhance the tramp-like image he wished to create. Inspired by the rag rugs he had helped his mother to make in his youth, Jim had cajoled his ever-patient wife to sew lengths of cast-off material onto old net curtains and create a tabard-like garment his dancers could wear with ease. It had been necessary to forage for extra material in charity shops but soon, a dozen costumes (spares included) had been completed by Jim's wife and the Raggy Men were born. Jim had pronounced the effect as:

"Perfect!"

Other less biased and unkind onlookers might have used the word;

"Ridiculous!"

Jim insisted his men provide pure white handkerchiefs of regulation size and quality and he had purchased sticks and bells. Today the troupe would perform. Jim had puffed out his chest with pride at the thought. The leaflet informed the public when the dancing would begin;

'Between 2 pm and 4 pm on the Upper Egginton Village Green, immediately after the completion of the Duck Race in the village stream.'

There had been many such invitations to dance outside The Green Man public house. After all, the owner and licensee, Tom King was a peripheral member of the Raggy Men. Tom was no great dancer and was disliked by many in the group but Jim had included him in his projects as a matter of expediency. In winter they could use his backroom for practice and whatever might be Tom's failings socially, all agreed his beer was the best in Shropshire. Tom would only be called on in the event of holidays or sickness in the group but even then, would not always be available when The Green Man was at its busiest. Tom for his part encouraged the Raggy's on the basis that he could call upon the dancers to perform on high days and holidays, did not need to pay them and their attraction ensured a full bar and lounge. Okay, there was the outlay of a couple of free rounds but that was minuscule compared to the increased profit and Tom was all for profit no matter who he needed to screw for it.

Today, with the extra entertainment of those old favourites; the duck race, scruffy dog competition and the Morris dancers, he was assured of a good day's takings providing the weather held fair. It was May in all its bud bursting glory. His cellar was bountifully stocked with real ale and draft locally brewed cider. It was the fare that brought in drinkers from the surrounding areas and much further afield.

Jim Walsh's men were as different as the proverbial chalk and cheese and it pleased his ego to imagine he and no one else could have brought them together and forged such a tight-knit group. There were accountants (both practicing and retired), farm labourers, retired doctors, a vet, an ex-army private, a mechanic and of course a publican. Apart from Tom King, this eclectic group got on well. Jim had made an exception to the qualifications required for a Raggy in the case of ex squaddie Stan Till. The man had returned from Iraq injured in both legs and was confined to a wheelchair. Nevertheless, Jim had seen something in him and concluded that it was his duty to help a man who had given much for his country. So it was that Stan was given the position of 'fool', and was required to manoeuvre his wheelchair in a circle around the Morris men as they danced. He rattled a stick loaded with bells and generally behaved like the village savant. His idiot cameo, together with his infirmity had proved highly successful and the bucket he clutched entreating watchers to 'Please give generously' provided a welcome addition towards the running costs of the Raggy Men with a little leftover for local charities.

Chapter 3

Tom King watched the pints flow, watched the money flow, and was on guard for sticky-fingered staff. Part-time youngsters came and went and part-time youngsters sometimes exited The Green Man more quickly than they expected. On one occasion, a part-time youngster ended his day in A & E in Bridgnorth Hospital. Tom knew all the ruses and he was wont to act speedily and without warning in the event of theft in its many guises. The old adage of there being nothing new under the sun shone brightly as far as Tom King was concerned. He was heard to advise some miscreant who lay cowering in the village gutter;

"Son, I invented that one so don't try it on with the master"

He had a couple of long-serving barmaids who he trusted and a man in his mid-twenties who, despite a dubious past could be called upon for cellar work, brewery work and to assist behind the bar. For what he paid him, Tom reckoned it was worth the gamble.

Tom was something of a ladies' man and tended to recruit by looks rather than ability. He oozed an excess of testosterone from every pore and the man made no attempt to hide his needs. Tom and his wife, Bella, shared the ownership of The Green Man on a fifty-fifty basis. Their marriage was far less balanced. Bella King was in her mid-thirties, several years younger than her husband and attractive in a dark Latino kind of way. Her figure was voluptuous, the eyes stunningly dark and she still wore her long hair loose unless working in the small back room which the Kings had converted into a kitchenette. Food was basic and the preparation areas just about passed the Food Hygiene Inspector's regular scrutiny. The range of food produced was simple: cheese cobs, cheese and onion cobs; bacon lettuce and tomato cobs or sausage butties. A pan full of chips constantly sizzled on the barely adequate stove Tom made no money out of these but it was necessary to at least provide snacks in the modern pub trade.

Many suggested that it was not the food that encouraged sales but the opportunity for the local menfolk to ogle the 'Missus'. She in turn played up to the locals. Oddly, none of the wives seemed to take umbrage and, in any case, Bella King, though revelling in the attention was for business reasons strict about where she drew the line, unlike (as many were heard to mutter) her husband.

It was the weekend of The Fun Day. The Green Man was heaving with jostling punters both male and female. There was a regular movement of trays holding pints, glasses of red wine or pop and crisps for the kids. Crowds pressed through the small doorway and out onto the beer garden overlooking the village green where smokers smoked and others coughed exaggeratedly, pointedly waving away the smoke.

Mr. Whippy played an out-of-tune music box version of The Blue Danube. Grownups queued; children went on tiptoe to order their favourites impatiently waiting for their parents to pay. Ice creams coated the faces of the very young whilst others demanded replacements after seeing the source of their current pleasure melt and fall onto the grass at their feet.

A woman from the local hospice was selling raffle tickets for a draw that would take place in a month's time. Tom King's bar staff were selling Green Man masks, purchased in bulk and sold with a substantial mark-up.

The duck race was strictly controlled by the local Arkela, leader of Upper and Lower Eggington Brownies aided by several little girls looking cute in brown uniforms. All ducks had been bet upon and a handsome amount raised for the maintenance work needed on the Brownie coach. There were problems however as the brook was at a low ebb and the number of ducks sold was far in excess of what realistically could be expected to bob along to the finish line. Arkela's branch, snapped off from an overhanging willow tree, soon had them progressing towards victory, yellow bodies moving unsteadily with the flow, orange beaks bowing to those on the bank shouting for their favourites.

Next appeared several rather mangy-looking canines, lined up, some growling, some totally disinterested, waiting to be judged by a local councillor. Tails wagged, treats were eaten and owners brushed their adored dogs. The sight of a black and white Jack Russell slipping his collar and disappearing into a thicket, its owner sliding on the wet grass and ending up in an untidy heap, brought a huge roar from the crowd. King had been asked to judge the competition but his excuse had been:

"Sorry, a gaffer can't show preference in football, politics, religion, or hairy dogs."

After much discussion and inspection from a safe distance, the councillor had selected the winner, lineage unknown but giving the distinct impression to the crowd that one bite might ensure the unlucky recipient risking a nasty bout of hydrophobia.

The Raggy Men Morris dancers were preparing for their entrance. The possibility of a last-minute hitch was always a worry as the Raggy Men had a considerable following and a nonappearance would have been akin to Bono cancelling an appearance at the V Festival.

All was well; the troupe was ready, limbering up in the backroom of The Green Man; some nervous, some relishing another public appearance. Stan Till's motorised wheelchair was secreted to the side of the pub. A few children had spotted him and were sniggering at this strange apparition, moving gently forward, careful not to snag his ragged outfit in the wheels of his machine. A couple of musicians, one with fiddle, and the other with accordion were practising chords. They would lead the procession of dancers onto the green.

Jim Walsh in his role as 'the squire,' checked out his men's bell pads, baldrics, rosettes and sashes and of course the rags so essential for any self-respecting Raggy Man. The crier meanwhile bawled out the virtues of the dancers as fiddle and accordion started up with 'Trinkles' a tune much loved by Jim. Stan had driven his machine around the circle marked out for the dance and proceeded to wave his hands and gurn, jaw and tongue rolling and teeth grinding grotesquely much to the amusement of the watching public. Stan was the warm-up act and the man whose success in shaking the donations bucket was vital for the group's finances.

Way up above in the cloudless blue, the balloons released by children in the hope of winning a teddy in the balloon race floated serenely onwards. Sadly, several hapless blue-coloured deflated inflatables ended their flights hanging from tree branches much to the dismay of their young owners.

Hours later, a delighted Jim sat beaming at his troupe in the snug; pints of King's Best Bitter had been downed as evidenced by rows of empty pint glasses and foamy beards. The conversation was becoming loud, bawdy and even the worst joke resulted in gales of laughter and glasses being banged on tables in appreciation.

Chapter 4

Back in Anglo-Saxon times, what was now Upper Egginton was a place of worship due to the fate of a Christian priest unlucky enough to be in the wrong place at the wrong time. Father Egbert of Bridgnorth had, so legend had it, wandered into the woods which then covered the current site of the village at just about the same time as a longship full of marauding Vikings had beached after making its way up the Severn. The priest had been tied to a roughly made wooden cross, floated out onto the river, and was used by carousing Danes for target practice. Just as the first arrow was about to be launched, the previously lowering sky opened and a shaft of sunlight shone down blinding the bowmen. For several minutes, none could see the river and by the time they were back in focus, both priest and raft had disappeared.

Father Egbert was never seen again and the usual rumours were circulated. He had, it was said, been whisked off to heaven still attached to the cross. The whole episode had proved in modern parlance a nice little earner for locals who began to build temporary hovels in the area of the miracle and sell touristy trinkets to pilgrims. Eventually, capitalism and religion melded into one and were so successful that a church and stone cottage for the clergy were built. So it was that Upper Egginton came into being.

The Green Man owed its origin to its position on what used to be a drovers' path. No one knew whether this was by design or just a fortuitous accident. Weary men would stay awhile, shake off the dust of the road and examine their blistered and bloody feet. There was the urgent need to slake their thirst before once more moving their sheep to the marshalling yards on the Severn or making a further journey to Wolverhampton. Many areas of that city still bore the title of 'folds' and a 'wool sack' was incorporated in the coat of arms. This early incarnation of an alehouse was part of the commercial enterprise of local monks. After the Reformation, brewing fell into the hands of local entrepreneurs, Tom and Bella King being the latest owners.

A never-ending supply of uncontaminated water from a spring at the rear made the pub an ideal place for brewing. Brewers at The Green Man had always purchased local malted barley and following the addition of hops in the Middle Ages, locally grown hops from the many hop yards were available in the region. The yeast used in fermentation continued, generation after generation, and the fungus was cosseted and cared for.

Tom King's small brewery maintained the traditions and brews of his predecessors and added a few more on special occasions. To Tom, terms such as mash tun, fermenters and racking were in everyday use. Tom King cared very little for those around him but his beer making was something he cherished. Certainly, he enjoyed the wealth that his art provided but he basked also in the compliments which rained down upon him for his ale. Women and ale; ale and women, that was the span of much of King's life but with one addition; money. Money was important. The by-products of the process were sold for cattle feed, or fertiliser and excess yeast was sold to a health food shop for conversion into yeast tablets.

The Raggy Men were at that stage of beer consumption where they were demanding yet another trip around the brewery. 'Complete fools,' he thought. Just look at them. Most were still wearing their costumes. Attempts to avoid the brewery visit were all to no avail. Tom was busy and, in any case, all he needed was for some idiot to spew up into the mash tun or slip and break a leg. Still, they were perhaps his consistently best customers, so grudgingly he led the swaying troupe to the rear of the pub and up the slatted wooden stairway. They jostled and grabbed at each other, slapped backs, and generally behaved like children in a school playground. Tom was relieved that the climbing of stairs had been completed without mishap. Patiently he took them through the processes. None seemed to show interest, it was a means to an end. Someone shouted:

"Where's the free beer, Tom?"

The thought; 'Morons!' echoed in Tom's mind as he ignored the raucous comments. He breathed a silent sigh of relief as he escorted the last Raggy Man back the way they had come and down the stairway. It was necessary to tend to his ales and he needed peace. He locked both doors into his brewery and looked about him, Tom the king surveying his domain. He was not aware that his actions were being observed.

Chapter 5

Tom King was going through his checks. He was pleased to see that the next brew was fermenting nicely. The temperature necessary in order to grow the yeast was being maintained, too cold and the yeast would not ferment, too hot and it might die. Barm was a living organism and Tom cosseted it lovingly. He had converted what had been a primitive brewhouse into a small modern microbrewery beloved by every Campaign for Real Ale enthusiast. There was nothing of the homebrew about King's operation. Many made the journey to worship at the shrine of King's Beers and in his bar, he exhibited his CAMRA certificate;

'Best pub in the West Midlands 2016.'

He cultivated that society in the same way as he cultivated any who might add to The Green Man's profits, adding to his current welfare and bolstering his ever-growing pension fund.

King enjoyed his brewery but at some time, he would have to accept that age would mean that the physical effort necessary would bring an end to his involvement. The false bonhomie with customers or his threats to the unruly would eventually catch up with him. The carefully cultivated facade of 'Mine Host' was a daily chore that went against his whole character. Beneath the exterior, there lay a festering hate for what he regarded as 'country bumpkins, bloody turnip heads'. Where he had lived most of his life and the way he had lived it would be totally alien to these people he thought. Furthermore, many were jealous of his success, and most regarded him as a 'Johnny come lately' in the village.

"How long does it take to be accepted in this bloody village? Am I always to be regarded as an 'outcomer'?" he would ask.

Bella would merely smile. She knew that he would never be regarded as truly a member of the community. She had inherited what was then a derelict building; roofless, with every windowpane, broken or cracked and ivy devouring the brickwork. She had also received within the will the extensive land surrounding the ruin but this had been deemed relatively worthless and unsuitable for any kind of farming.

There had been much gossip in the village as to how young Bella Everley had returned from London with a man in tow and a wedding ring on her finger. Here was a young woman who was not only beautiful, an ex-Miss Bridgnorth a few years previously but who also it was rumoured, had gained a first in Economics at Cambridge. When she had moved south to take up a position in The City, the locals had never expected to see her in Upper Eggington again and her inheritance had returned to its natural state. New waves of weeds, nettles and convolvulus ruled the land and invaded buildings. Metal mesh fences adorned with signs warning, 'Danger keep out' were erected around The Green Man.

Tom King was introduced to all and sundry as her husband and she was now Mrs Bella King. There was no doubt that the man was handsome, had the physique of a professional sportsman and adopted informal, smart but casual attire. Ties and lounge suits were not for this man. He exuded a kind of physical magnetism that soon won over the ladies of the village. Not so however the men and the sense of jealousy was indeed palpable. Here was some southerner, with an accent from somewhere 'down there', who it seemed wives and daughters found attractive and who was married to a woman who many of the locals had unsuccessfully tried to date in the past. Still, they had to grudgingly admit, the man was industrious and soon phoenix-like, The Green Man arose and was once more the village pub it had been years previously. In fact, he was so successful that its fame grew throughout that part of Shropshire.

Once brewing had begun and life was once more breathed into the community, many accepted King but even more, would never accept him into their society. When men assembled to gossip or watch a local football match, it was whispered darkly that there was something about the man but that they just could not put their finger on what it was. His attempt at integration involved encouraging Women's Institute Meetings in the pub, fetes, Sunday school treats, and school sports days in his fields.

When the necessary reroofing project was undertaken for the pub, he met the householders of the half dozen houses in the attached terrace and suggested that the block might be retiled in total and that he would bear a part of their costs. This was universally accepted. On the face of it, the deal was a good one but many whispered that King had received 'back handers' which more than compensated for his subsidising the venture.

Most believed that King had financed the pub's renaissance and that his contribution had enabled him to become an equal partner with Bella. Once more, the knowledge of the man's financial stake in the business only added to the dislike of King.

Chapter 6

"Tom, we need you down here, the bitter's just gone. Can you change onto the next barrel please?"

There was no reply from the brewery; just an echo bouncing off ancient walls and Bella King knew that to trespass into Tom's area would not be taken kindly.

"Tom, for God's sake! We're up to our eyes in it down here and I can't take Dean off the bar."

There was still no answer and she stamped away huffily back into the lounge. Bella had received no response an hour later and had been forced to leave her kitchen duties and work the bar whilst Dean changed the barrels in the cellar. By this time, a red mist had descended upon her usually unruffled consciousness and once Dean was again serving the customers, she retrieved the brewery key from its hook at the rear of the bar, jiggled it in the lock and pushed at the door.

As had been the situation on many occasions, there would be words passed between Mr. and Mrs. King. She knew that this might result in more than four- letter expletives thrown in her direction. Often, she had been on the end of a thrown fist, as had been the case a day or so ago but really, this was too much.

The door did not give. Either something had blocked the entrance or has had often been the case, King had bolted the door from the inside when he did not wish to be disturbed. Bella took a kick at the door, turned, and once more stomped back into the bar, her usual amiable self unable to disguise her annoyance to all and sundry at what had happened. A young couple sucking their way through cocktails in the snug looked up and were surprised to see the anger on Bella King's face.

Dean Jones, a twenty-three-year-old, ex-offender who Tom King had employed was aware of her mood immediately. There might be a decade's difference in their ages but Dean had always placed Mrs. King on a pedestal and she had been the sole reason he had remained at The Green Man. Deep inside there boiled resentment towards Tom King which in different circumstances would have resulted in him assaulting the publican. It had been a long day in The Green Man and Dean had been part of it from start to finish. He could have taken an hour's break during the early afternoon but Mrs King was struggling so apart from a brief excursion onto the village green and a breath of fresh air, he would stay and help. Anyway, what was that bastard Tom King doing? Normally he'd be directing things when there was a full house. Not like him to play the wallflower when things were going so well. Tom King needed to be 'front of house' acting the part he played so well.

Bella King rang the closing time bell, sighed, and once more tried the brewery door. The result was the same. Her mood had changed and her annoyance had turned to a creeping feeling in the pit of her stomach that all was not well. She called to Dean for assistance.

"Leave the bar to Tracey, Dean; I think we have a problem back here."

She signalled to Dean that he should carefully lever open the door. She had not the courage to insist that he smash the door. Bella knew what her husband's reaction would be to that. Dean applied a wrench to the hinges and gradually the door began to open as bolts were eased from their fixings.

"Let me go up first Bella, just in case he's drunk or something."

Bella King knew her husband would not be the worse for drink. That was for his customers but not for him.

Dean gasped, both horrified and unable to accept what he was seeing. King's body seemed almost to be examining the contents of stainless steel Fermenting Vessel 3 (FV3). The motors gave off a steady hum and the contents softly pulsated. The yeast made gentle bubbling noises and peaks and troughs morphed second by second into different shapes. Crests gave an almost dirty brown appearance whilst troughs remained creamy white. The naked torso was draped half in, half out of FV3. The feet and legs straddled the side; the head and upper body were hidden from view within the vessel. Dean lent against a stanchion, breathed in deeply, and attempted to take control.

"Better stay down there Mrs King. Could you phone for the police and an ambulance, your husband's had an accident."

Bella King, however, was made of sterner stuff and before Dean could prevent her, she had squeezed by him and was looking down at the prone body of Tom King. She maintained an icy exterior and walked back towards her barman. There was still not the slightest flicker of emotion.

"Too late for an ambulance Dean. I'll phone the police."

Chapter 7

DCI Ben Pitt and his assistant DS Jaswinder Khunkhun, known to all as 'Jaz' had received an early morning call from the police station at Bridgnorth. It meant crossing into West Mercia's patch and Pitt baulked at the prospect. This would usually have resulted in angry exchanges; the usual 'keep off our turf' but on this occasion, the Force was fully involved in a major police operation. The pair had been up most of the night on a fairly routine domestic assault case but the urgency of the call meant that sleep must wait for later. At about six a.m. they were approaching the gash slashed out of the red sandstone cliff to create the road that zigzagged down into Bridgnorth. Known locally as the Hermitage, the views towards the two-tiered settlement of High Town and Low Town were spectacular. They crossed the old stone bridge over the sluggish brown waters of the Severn and past the sign which read 'Welcome to Historic Bridgnorth.' The Busy Lizzies, begonias and petunias in the wrought iron displays were at their early summer best. Dewdrops, soon to disappear with the coming of the day's warmth glistened on fresh green leaves and vibrant petals. In a few months, the flowers would tire, fade and the flashy riot of colour would disappear. For now, locals and tourists could admire the display's beauty and breath in the perfumes.

Khunkhun took a left turn after crossing the bridge and obeyed the lady's bluestocking voice issuing directives from his sat-nav. He drove up the hill and past the entrance to the Severn Valley Railway. Down below him, he could see that several locomotives were being made ready for the expected influx of Sunday tourists. Steam issued from unseen funnels and the chug, chug sound of steam engines filled the air. Now and then a shrill hoot was heard. Soon they were deep into the Shropshire countryside and driving along narrow winding roads totally unknown to Khunkhun. Pitt cursed as they were forced to slow down to a walking pace after rounding a bend and finding their path restricted by a council hedge and tree trimming machine. Eventually, they were waved past at a lay-by. By now the sun floated, an orange ball on the horizon, winking on and off through the hedgerows. The early morning mist had burned off and high above, a passenger jet's vapour trail first streaked the cloudless sky and then dissolved. On the distant hills, a smudge of trees was outlined against the azure whilst in a nearby field, a small group of brown cows grazed serenely beside a muddy water hole.

Pitt, eyes closed, trying to insert his frame into a position that might give just a smidgeon of comfort opened an eye, glanced at the scene, and murmured:

"What am I doing heading to God knows where to investigate the murder of some turnip grower when I could be out for a pleasant round of golf Jaz?"

His experiences both as a rookie cop and during the upward climb to his present status had created in his mind a cynical ambivalent response to murder. On the one hand, he was still appalled at the level of violence so-called civilised man was capable of whilst at the same time regarding such acts in the same way as he viewed war. In both cases, these were not aberrations but more the normal and expected way that society would always behave.

"Well firstly sir, he's a publican and secondly, you don't play golf and in fact, you are normally scathing about anyone who does. I'd be prepared to swear under oath that you even suggested that the Chief Constable's Annual Charity Golf Bash was a right load of golf balls."

"Mmm fair comment Jaz. Guilty as charged but you know what I mean."

He continued in somnolent mode. A smile eased its way across his still handsome features as he remarked;

"On reflection, I might just take it up when I retire. All my contemporaries seem to spend their entire lives on the course. I guess there may be something in the bloody game apart from walking miles across fields come rain, come shine."

They were taking a route vaguely parallel to the River Severn. The patchwork of fields had been laid out seemingly by some long dead artist who had then coloured them in using green, gold or oilseed rape yellow. The morning brought more vehicles out on the road and they were forced to squeeze the car against the hedgerows. Khunkhun fully expected that his route lady might mischievously lead them up some dirt track to nowhere and he was relieved when eventually she advised:

"Take the next turning on the right and then after a quarter of a mile you will arrive at your destination."

Pitt yawned, stretched himself and muttered,

"Thank you! We've been at it an hour and a half."

Madam Satnav's directions were accurate and a narrow lane widened out to reveal a smallish hamlet of perhaps fifty or so dwellings, a village green, pub and church. A stream trickled lazily through the sedge grass making its lonely way to Pitt thought; God alone knows where. The village was blooming in its extravagant efforts to win the annual 'Shropshire in Bloom' competition and colour was everywhere. Pitt could not remember seeing so many hanging baskets all in one small area. When he had been married, one of his wives, (he could not now remember which) had insisted on him making an effort in the garden. He had spent hours creating several hanging baskets prior to valiant attempts to drill and screw brackets into walls; a DIY effort which proved only partially successful. In any case, the rooted plugs he had planted had not lived long enough to actually create a display and he had been nagged for months whilst the long dead corpses of petunias blew in the wind. Some have green fingers, some do not he thought. The church bells rang, animated ladies in Sunday hats and Sunday suits seemed to be buzzing like bees whilst their menfolk in uniformly dark suits and ties indulged in more subdued discussions.

"Bloody hell Jaz! It seems we are entering a time warp here. I seem to remember this scene when I was a kid. Surely there must be a field full of scarecrows around here somewhere and a bunch of straw-sucking yokels prodding strangers with their pitchforks?"

"I don't know guv, it's the kind of place my granddad dreamt of when he left the army to settle in what he always called 'The Mother Country'. Pity there's no thatched roofs; granddad had a big thing about thatched roofs. He had half a dozen pictures of thatched cottages around the house with of course loads of rambling roses just to complete things. You must admit, it does give the impression of some children's storybook ending with, "and they all lived happily ever after."

Jaz was aware that in the event, granddad had settled alongside eight other immigrants in a two up two down condemned slum in Whitmore Reans, a suburb of Wolverhampton. He'd got himself a job as a bus conductor. In the Forties and Fifties, there were jobs aplenty and granddad's next battle turned out to be with the corporation bus company over his beard and turban. Granddad won and insisted on maintaining those parts of his Sikh identity which he regarded as sacrosanct. At the time of his death, his pure white beard flowed down to his waist. Many of his friends of a similar age wore their uncut beards tied beneath their chin in the manner first demanded of Sikhs in the previous century when joining the British Army, but not Granddad. As he was often heard to say;

"They think they're working for the Raj and worry about setting their beards on fire or getting them caught in the mechanism when firing a gun. Bloody fools, don't they understand we are all Brits now in a free country."

"You just don't expect this kind of crime in places like this guv", Jaz said.

Pitt merely grunted and shook his head. As far as he was concerned, sewers flowed even in Utopia and idyllic or not, heinous crimes would still be committed. The only difference in the perps was class or accent.

Much to the chagrin of his parents and his other siblings, Jaz cared little about his heritage and was totally westernised. At gatherings; births, deaths etc. he would never consciously seek to embarrass his family and would try to conform but that was the full extent of his involvement. He was ambitious, a man fully intent on bettering himself. In spite rather than because of the teachers, he had achieved 'A' and 'A+' levels before leaving from a none too excellent comprehensive school; paid his own way through university as a part-time barman or taxi driver and managed a couple of firsts in law and economics.

He knew his fast-tracking in the police force was the cause of much jealousy amongst colleagues but his successful partnership with Pitt had done much to silence his critics. Khunkhun had manoeuvred his promotions so that his ultimate aim of working with one of the most respected officers in the West Midlands could be fulfilled.

DCI Ben Pitt was wedded to 'The Force'. It was and always would be his life and he sometimes thought ruefully; 'his wife'. He had often remarked that a man can only have one successful marriage and pointed to the fact that he had two failed marriages as proof of this. Pitt recalled that his first wife had an endless passion for shiny blingy jewellery and he well remembered accidentally opening her jewellery box one sunny day only to be temporarily blinded as if he were in the scene from Indiana Jones when the Ark of the Covenant was opened. It was a wake-up call. His life had to change.

His second wife had during one of the many spats remarked that she had always thought of herself as having an affair with him rather than being his wife. Ben Pitt was ruggedly handsome, square-jawed, middle-aged and six feet tall. He still had the physique of a man perhaps a decade younger and could still destroy opponents half his age on the squash court. Having a reputation for self-control in taut situations, he had earned the respect of his peers. It was only when those deep blue eyes flashed out a warning that fellow officers or some villain needed to beware of his inner passion.

Jaz brought the Jaguar to a crunching slithering stop on the gravel forecourt of The Green Man Public House. He set the handbrake, turned off the ignition, left the car in gear, and after slamming the door and followed Pitt to the entrance. Partially hidden amongst the ivy which had over the years sought to claim the entrance as well as the walls, the black metal plaque read:

'Thomas King, licensed to sell all intoxicating liquor for consumption on or off these premises.'

Khunkhun noted a brave rambling rose still managing to survive in this forest of ivy. The blooms were few but the many buds suggested the possibility of a fine display later in the season. Okay granddad, sorry but that's the best we can do he mused.

Chapter 8

Outside The Green Man, a bored uniformed officer slouched; head cocked speaking into his shoulder radio. On seeing the DCI, the officer finished his conversation abruptly. Pitt nodded to him. Many in the CID regarded the boys in 'tit helmets'; the 'wooden tops' as an inferior breed, necessary but not to be treated as equal. Pitt had never subscribed to this and as a result was respected by the uniformed officers in much the same way as he was somewhat grudgingly within his own branch.

Pitt and Khuhkhun entered into the darkness and made for the light at the top of the stairs. The place had a delicious aroma of malt and hops. Arc lights gave off an unearthly white illumination. SOCOs busied themselves, wearing protective suits and masks and giving the impression that they were about to quote, "One small step for man" rather than investigating a murder. Various areas had been identified with coloured markers and patches of white powder indicating where fingerprints had been found. Cameras flashed recording that moment in time at the crime scene. Bryn Edwards looked up from his notebook, scrawled a word and beamed at Pitt.

"Good to see you again Pitt. Pint later? They tell me the beer's absolute nectar not like that gnat's piss lager your young apprentice drinks."

Edwards, the foremost forensic pathologist in the region, always gave the impression that he lived for his job and relished a good murder in the same way as a trencherman relished a cordon bleu meal. Today must be something really special thought Pitt; the man's positively beaming.

"What is it today, Bryn? Patches, E. Cigs, gum?"

"Taking no bloody chances Pitt. Doing the lot and I've got a packet of Bensons as a fallback."

"You just might crack it then Bryn. So, what have we here?"

Shortly, the body would be enclosed in a zipped black bag in readiness for removal. Plastic bags would have been taped around wrists prior to this, enclosing each hand in order to preserve any evidence. Pitt had been on hand at many autopsies and always prepared himself mentally for the fetid smell; the stainless steel dissection table and the rubber body block placed under the neck of the naked corpse. Pitt made a point of skipping breakfast prior to his witnessing the procedures. There were the ever-present sounds of dissection, the vibrating Stryker saw used on the skull and the crunch as a cap like portion was levered off. He would turn away as a Y shaped incision was made from the shoulder joint to meet mid chest and continue down to the pubic region. As with many professionals, Bryn used garden sheers when cutting ribs. The slopping sound as brain, heart and organs were stored and preserved in individual jars, always resulted in queasiness. Even Vaseline applied to the nostrils, which supposedly made the reek easier to bear, had little effect when an autopsy had been performed following the disinterment of a body. Pitt would be supplied with scrubs and a hairnet but even so, the return to his normal clothes always seemed to result in the vile stench being sucked into the fabric. Dry cleaning for outerwear and hot machine washes for the rest of one's clothing was imperative after completing that part of his work.

Bryn Edwards enjoyed what he described as his art. ('Yes Pitt this is an art as well as a science.') After years working in the Black Country, he had endeavoured to lose his 'Valleys' accent realising that publicising his Welsh origins might be a disadvantage. However, when discussing matters with the DCI, he would flip a switch, knowing that this would annoy Pitt.

"Well boyo, if you can just observe procedure, slip into the nitrile gloves or maybe you've brought your Marigolds with you? and find yourself a size twelve pair of booties, I'll escort you on a conducted tour of my crime scene."

The officers had already collected the necessary protection and proceeded to don gloves and footwear. They moved closer to the corpse better to observe the bizarre scene now confronting them.

"May I draw your attention to the following: One; written in some kind of black pen on the side of the vessel we have a quote from I believe, 'The Emperor's New Clothes':

'THE KING IS IN THE ALLTOGETHER.'

This I assume applies to Mr. King here who as is written, is very definitely 'in the altogether!' Stark bollock naked one might say. Two; if you take a look to the side here, we have an empty wallet, the contents of which you will see floating on the surface of the white stuff which as you know is balm used in the making of beer. We have a selection of plastic cards and fivers, tenners and twenties. I guess there's about a hundred and fifty quid in there. Dirty money, a tip for the cleaning lady, or maybe some dark message?"

He dragged a finger into the brew, examined the resultant white scum as if searching for a clue, then wiped it on his overalls before continuing.

"Let us now come to the vexed question as to why the landlord of this noble establishment should seek to pursue his trade stark naked and examining his brew so closely that he's halfway immersed in it. You will also see that in addition to this, he is wearing what I am told by one of the locals is a Green Man mask, back to front. So we have him face forward looking at his brew whilst he wears a mask that looks directly at us. One might use the expression 'two-faced'. Maybe this is some local tradition whereby brewers do their work naked and wearing a mask. A little unlikely you may say. But enough of tradition, let me lead you to the facts of the case. He did not drown in his own rather fine ale, nor was he throttled. No sign of any pinpoint haemorrhages around the eyes; no petechiae. So what we ask caused this sudden demise? Well let me show you what I'm guessing is the cause. I've saved the best for you Pitt"

Edwards bent over the body and with some difficulty, carefully removed the mask to reveal a wound, circular in shape and about two inches in diameter. The exact shape could not be accurately assessed as blood and brain matter encrusted the skull. The mixture had acted as a kind of glue matting the hair to The Green Man mask. Strands of hair remained attached. The immersion in the liquid in the fermentation vessel had not as yet washed away the evidence.

"This my friends is a classic example of death resulting from blunt force trauma, possibly the most common type of injury encountered by the practising forensic pathologist. And why am I confident that this is the case you ask? Well, I'll save you detective types the problem of trying to work it out. So here covered in gore I present you with the rubber mallet used to stave in the licensee's head. This is a tool normally used to ensure the bung is safely installed in the cask and ironically, what would normally be used to prevent leakage of beer has here been used to create leakage of brain matter."

Edwards puffed out his ex-rugby player's ample chest and assumed the smug facial expression of a man who is confident that he knows more than the next. Pitt turned to Khunkhun.

"As ever Jaz, this Welsh Wizard has solved yet another case for us."

Bryn ignored the comment and continued,

"Let us now discuss the mask. You will see that it is cheap cardboard and is designed to give the impression that branches bearing fruit have sprouted from the face whilst leaves grow from the ears. What the hell is this supposed to be? Well, I will tell you. This is a representation of The Green Man from whom this establishment takes its name. I am told by one of the locals that legend has it that in the churchyard there resides the actual Green Man, twigs leaves and all buried six feet down in the earth."

"Fascinating stuff Bryn, they just don't pay you enough."

"How very true! I try not to bore when communicating such vital information Pitt and by the way, here's another conundrum for you and Dr. Watson. They had to break down the door to get in. It was locked and bolted from the inside. I've no idea how some man or maybe woman got in, smashed his head in and got out. Very Agatha Christie. 'Murder in the locked brewery' perhaps?

Khunkhun had been examining the door. "It's true enough sir but I guess if we have a look around, there's probably a simple explanation."

"Well good luck with that one Jaz. There's no bloody windows and not even a chimney for Santa Claus to climb down and do the deed. Well, must get on, not much left for you boys to do. Practically solved the case for you. Obviously, some bloody psychopath"

"Mmmm let's hope my ex-wife has an alibi then Bryn."

Pitt turned to leave. Khunkhun followed.

Chapter 9

Mrs King was as Khunkhun observed later, "Quite a stunner." Jennifer Lopez came instantly to mind. Mid-thirties, her long shiny hair was cut in a modern shaggy irregular line giving her a slightly gipsy appearance. Whilst working, she wore a flowery tabard and a pair of skin tight jeans. The DCI was he would admit to himself, a man susceptible to the allure of beautiful women and aware that he had to be on guard in the current situation. The old advice about never mixing work with pleasure was certainly applicable when dealing with Bella King.

She did not display the normal characteristics of a woman whose husband had been murdered within the preceding twenty-four hours and who had been first on the scene to witness the macabre way he had met his end. When Pitt and Khunkhun entered the lounge, they were surprised to find that she was making preparations for reopening the pub. Whilst a young man cleared glasses, a woman who Pitt assumed to be a barmaid cleaned tabletops and Mrs King busied herself checking levels in the spirit dispensers. All seemed perfectly normal, just another trading day in The Green Man.

Mrs. King turned as they approached and displayed a welcoming smile. The voice was sensual, low and husky.

"I assume you wish to question me regarding my husband's death? One moment and we can talk privately in my office."

Not a flicker of grief, no noticeable signs of unhappiness on her strikingly beautiful face. Mrs King was it seemed, a very calm and composed widow indeed. The cleaning woman signalled to her that she had finished the tables. She waved a dripping floor mop in Mrs King's direction.

"Just doing the toilets now Bella unless there's something else on?"

"Oh no Ethel, once you've finished the ladies and the gents, that's all for now and I'll see you for the evening shift. Dean will be okay for lunchtime, if (and she turned to Pitt) the officers here allow us to open the doors? Dean would you mind bringing coffee and a few biscuits up to my office please?"

Dean gave her an adoring glance; a tail-wagging puppy wishing to please its mistress as he made his way into the kitchen.

The office was totally functional. Pitt and Khunkhun, pulled out a couple of hardbacked office chairs whilst Mrs King swung her elegant legs and swivelled around on her faux black leather executive chair. As she scooted herself forward, Pitt noted a pair of expensive-looking deep red stiletto heeled shoes. The officers introduced themselves formally.

"Just one moment gentlemen. I must change. This one's for the washing basket."

Bella made great play of removing her tabard and heaving a sigh, flung the garment into an open rattan laundry basket. The dark blue cable knit sweater she wore emphasized her movie-star figure. Pursing her 'bee-stung' lips, she gave a sigh. "That's more comfortable. Would you like to start now Mr Pitt or shall we wait for coffee or perhaps you'd prefer a nip of one of the spirits from behind the bar? Maybe a little absinthe Mr. Pitt? As we are aware, absinthe makes the heart grow fonder?"

Pitt could have sworn she gave him a wink but maybe not.

"I'd like to get started if you don't mind Mrs King."

He was rewarded with a coquettish smile and a tossing of her long lustrous hair.

"Oh please, Mr Pitt; Bella."

Pitt was momentarily thrown off his stride. Khunkhun judged that to be the lady's objective. This was only momentary and Pitt explained that the discussion was informal but should she wish legal presence that would be her prerogative.

"Oh no, that will not be necessary. I don't actually have much to say anyway."

As she turned from the partial light of the office into the multifaceted glare of the sunlight arrowing through a cracked window, the officers were aware that a swelling on her right cheekbone had been skilfully disguised with makeup. Mrs King had obviously recently received a blow of some kind. Pitt spoke.

"Pardon me for remarking Mrs King ....Bella, but you seem to be taking your husband's murder very coolly."

For the first time, her expression changed, eyes narrowing, mouth just a little less smiling.

"A terrible thing yes, my reaction to this may be explained because Tom and I have not had the traditional man and wife relationship for several years. Ours is or was, purely a business relationship. I've lost a business partner, not a husband. He looked after the beer and organised functions whilst I look after the punters and the bar staff. It worked but now I have to reformulate the business and that's the end of the matter. It may sound a bit stony to you but I'm trying to be honest. In any case, I guess you'll be interviewing people who will be only too happy to dig the dirt on our relationship or more interestingly on Tom's serial relationships with other women. What you need to understand Inspector is that Tom and I got married in something of a hurry. Within three weeks of him chatting me up at a club we were there in a registry office tying the knot with three of the girls from work as witnesses. For all of it, the man was a smooth bastard and boy could he dance! Then it was off to Shropshire. I never met any of his friends or relatives and never have since. Strange that. Big mistake on my part and I very soon realised it but hey, I was young and foolish."

"Well thank you for your openness, Bella. Tell me, you seem to have a bruise on your face. How did that happen?"

Her fingertips moved to the bruise and then with a theatrical flourish, she promptly waved the question away. Pitt was aware of perfectly manicured nails varnished in a colour matching her footwear. Bella King's responses resembled the florets of a dandelion. Blow the seed head and the seeds flutter prettily in the wind. Once they land however, the resultant weed is tough and resilient. She gave her responses lightly but they were nevertheless effective in their nature.

"Oh, just my clumsiness Inspector, a tumble down the cellar steps. Luckily Tom was there to help me so no damage was done apart from a little bruising."

The mention of her husband's name was delivered or rather spat out in a manner that left no doubt as to her feelings. In spite of her effort to disguise the bruise, the swelling gleamed purple through the camouflaging cosmetics. Bella King's makeup was covering something less innocent than just a fall in the cellar. At that moment, Dean Jones kicked the office door open and entered with a tray of coffee, milk, sugar, and an unopened roll of ginger biscuits. He made no attempt at hiding his distaste for the situation, slamming the tray down onto the office desk. Cups rattled and the packet of biscuits rolled from side to side. Pitt gained the impression of a man in his early twenties, with the usual tattooed arms and a gym-honed body. Dean was a similar height to himself and his pale blue eyes and fair hair gave him a somewhat Nordic appearance.

"All okay or anything else you need Bella? Need me to stay?"

Once more he flashed Bella King an adoring look

"Oh no Dean, that's fine. You can get back to the bar now and thanks."

Dean left, slamming the door.

"He's such a dear you know, worth his weight in gold,"

and then more seriously, Bella King leaned forward as though there was some deep secret she was about to disclose.

"Tom took him on when no one else would. Mmmm that was Tom for you...............gave him a second chance but then he wouldn't he? He came cheap which was always a great big plus in Tom's world. More importantly, I know I can rely on him and I shall promote him and unlike my husband, I intend to pay him what he's worth." There it was again, a little praise for her husband and then the acid.

Pitt asked, "What was the problem with Dean?"

He sensed an almost maternal note as Bella replied,

"The high spirits of youth inspector. When he was in his late teens, he put a man into the hospital. They'd both been drinking and it was one of those 'Are you looking at me?' moments we get in the pub trade. Alcohol and machismo, they just don't mix at all well. Anyway, he received a suspended sentence but everyone knew about it; it appeared in the local papers so no chance of finding a job; a thousand CVs, a thousand cold shoulders. He started using the pub, got friendly with Tom and it went on from there. He's been with us now for five years and we've never had any problems. He tends to be a bit overprotective, a bit too clingy with me but he's never tried anything on and anyway, it's good for a girl's ego. He's over ten years younger than me but I wouldn't describe him as my toy boy".

Bella poured the coffee with drawing room elegance, offered biscuits, and answered every question with confidence and a smile. Khunkhun watched for the 'tells' indicating a departure from a truthful answer. He did not detect any change in her behaviour or demeanour. Bella King would have made a superb poker player. Then she said, "Could we carry on the conversation in the bar, gents? I've got some very thirsty customers waiting for me, well two at least," she said with a smile. Pitt agreed but wondered why Dean could not be relied upon to look after the business.

Chapter 10

Pitt and Khunkhun were led into the bar by Bella. She promised to have a full list of the names of as many regulars as she could remember from the previous day and suggested that the officers have a pint each on the house. They accepted and settled down for a cheese cob and a pint of Green Man Bitter. Drinking on duty? The Force had paid lip service to that cliché when Pitt had first joined. In his early days, a single pint would have been considered abstemious in the extreme by many. Those days were gone and latterly officers were much more cautious in these Politically Correct days. A pint would be the maximum and under normal circumstances, Jaz would have kept to a soft drink. Pitt was aware that Bryn Edwards might join them at any time once his work in the brewery was complete. The man would not normally restrict his alcohol intake but a twenty-mile drive back to Wolverhampton meant that on this occasion, his liver would be treated with respect. His usual socialising involved taxis to and from whatever watering hole he had opted for. There would be a five-pound tip to the driver should Bryn require help finding the key to open his front door.

Pitt looked around him. The lunchtime bar trade so far would be insufficient to pay Dean's wages he thought. Though the weather was seasonally warm, Bella had lit the ornate Victorian open fire. Flames crackled and roared in the chimney like some angry bear. A couple of old men, farmers possibly dressed by Tramps R Us were huddled around the grate. By the look of the boots and the stains on their trousers, they had recently perhaps been at work in byre, cattle shed, pigsty, or wherever farmers in Upper Egginton spent their working days Pitt thought. He was not by any means a fan of country life. Pitt was a man of town and city, preferring footpaths and diesel fumes to yomps across fields and the smell of cattle dung. Bella King carried a tray of brimming pint glasses and as she passed the officers whispered,

"Regulars; they feel the cold, thin blood you know. They can't make it to the bar these days so they have waitress service. Still, they deserve it after a bit of part-time work."

And I bet they love it, Pit thought. The men had propped their walking sticks against a wall. Elderly man number one was petting a scabby looking mongrel. The dog rolled over onto its back, paws in the air, happy and contented as the man stroked its belly. Mrs King placed four pints on a nearby table, gave both men a hug and 'chucked' the dog under his collar. The men stared appreciatively at Bella King's retreating rear end, made obvious sexist comments, roared with laughter and then concentrated on their beer. She returned to the bar, poured herself a Coke and pulled up a chair beside the officers.

"I can leave it to Dean now. Billy and Zeckial are specials, bless 'em. In here regular as clockwork. Two pints each at lunchtime, two pints each on the evening, seven days a week. I just wish we had a few more like them."

Zeckial? Pitt mused that perhaps he had stumbled into an episode of 'The Archers' and was about to become a character in 'an everyday story of country folk.' He resumed his questioning.

"Bella, may I ask the obvious? Have you the slightest idea who might have killed your husband?"

She gave the inspector what his mother would have termed 'an old-fashioned look.'

"I think I've already given you the idea that he wasn't too popular with some of the local males Inspector. Very popular with the ladies though. Draw your own conclusions."

"But has there been anything recently to trigger such a violent response?"

She gave Pitt the impression that she was pondering whether to answer truthfully or to keep 'shtum' in the belief that 'hubby' got just what had been coming to him. Nevertheless, after a brief hiatus, she must he thought have come to the conclusion that if she didn't mention it, then half of the clientele of The Green Man would.

"Well, there was a bit of an incident a week or two ago. Joe Palin; he's a local farmer, came in one night absolutely livid. I bet you could have heard his teeth gnashing all over the pub. He'd totally lost it, elbowed his way through the crowd, slammed open the flap and marched right to the back of the bar. Before anyone had realised it, he had Tom around the neck, throttling the life out of him shouting that he'd 'Bloody kill him and feed him to his pigs'. Tom was no Mr. Puniverse inspector but he couldn't get free and it took three of the locals to pull the man off. They dragged him outside and he was shouting things like 'Stay away from my whore of a wife or you'll find yourself in the cemetery where you belong alongside The Green Man you f'ing bastard."

Threats to the landlord and a connection between references to The Green Man and the corpse wearing a mask. It all sounded too pat, too obvious but then 'domestics' often followed a very simple path.

The bar had been filling as they spoke and the officers were aware of the chinking of glasses and an uneven volume of voices, interspersed with screams of female laughter and shouts from the younger men as some risqué episode was related with the usual exaggeration. The retelling of Saturday night's adventures, sexual or otherwise by the local Young Turks was a rite of passage.

The early evening session would soon be in full swing. Pitt wondered how many men were celebrating the untimely death of Tom King. Were their ladies drowning their sorrows at his untimely death or were there many, used and cast aside by Tom King, quietly raising a glass in a toast to his passing?

"Nothing else comes to mind then Mrs King? "

"Not really. He always had some irate husband or other threatening him but Tom could always look after himself."

Unless struck from behind with a mallet Pitt thought.

"Right well I think we'll leave it there. We shall be setting up a portable incident room. It will be to one side of the pub and I'll ensure that it doesn't inconvenience you. There will of course be uniformed police on hand. We don't know the motive for the crime yet and until we do, we shall try to ensure the safety of yourself and the locals. If you could pass on your list to one of the officers, we can get on with our interviews."

There was a momentary fluttering of the eye lashes as Mrs King replied, "I'm sure I shall feel safe with all these fit young policemen around to prevent me from coming to any harm Mr Pitt and there will be no problem with the Portacabin." With that Bella King sashayed back to the bar.

The officers wormed their way through the drinkers and out into the fading afternoon sunshine. Black clouds were filling the sky. Windscreen wipers would be required on the journey back to Wolverhampton.

On one corner of the village green, gulls were throwing a party with yesterday's discarded half-eaten hot dogs. The old chap with the mangy dog was heading unsteadily towards a rusting mud-spattered Land Rover circa the late Nineteen-Sixties. Pitt smiled to himself thinking, "You're taking a chance mate, there's uniformed police in the locality ready to demand a random breath test to relieve the boredom". The man drove away. Pitt was not here to carry out tests for excess alcohol.

In the village, cars were being washed, waxed and vacuumed. Several ancient-looking householders were engaged in removing any weed which may have strayed into their flower gardens and a young man leaned against a lamppost puffing out clouds of fog from an electronic cigarette. Children played their games on the green; an eccentric fusion of football, rugby and tag was the order of the day. Little boys shouted; little girls screamed. All was as it ever was on a Sunday afternoon in Upper Egginton. Jaz glanced towards the church. Sunshine glistened on its arched windows resulting in the stained-glass depictions of Jesus, Mary and the disciples momentarily coming to life. A mobility scooter made its awkward faltering way through the lych gate. Pitt spotted Bryn's Jag. Edwards surely was not still at work in the brewery? More likely, he was swapping tall stories with the local wiseacres in the snug.

Chapter 11

Khunkhun had dispensed with the services of Madam Satnav and had instead asked the way before leaving The Green Man. It had been the correct decision. The track was tortuous and the various zigzags and detours could never have been explained by a mere computer. Now and then, a sign warned that sheep, cows or deer might be crossing the road and therefore, the motorist needed to be alert to this. Pitt was just relieved that a colony of protected Natterjack toads had not made a home in that part of the county.

The detectives were greeted by a vicious looking mongrel with a goodly mix of Pitt Bull in its DNA. True to form, it growled, slobbered and flashed rows of teeth giving the appearance of having the capability to bite through solid steel should the need arise. The officers were careful to enter the farm fully twenty feet away from the muscular straining body which was now giving the appearance of being about to snap its taut heavy chain.

Pitt was not in the best of humour.

"Great parking Jaz."

Pitt had stepped out into a huge mound of animal excrement. The origin was unknown in this corner of Shropshire where animals seemed to hold sway over humans. His favourite Gucci loafers would never look or smell the same again. Together with women, clothes were yet another of the DCI's weaknesses. In The Great Western pub, a favourite with the local constabulary, he would often be referred to behind his back as: 'That flash bugger in the Armani suit with the Paki sidekick.' 'Positive discrimination!' was a phrase also frequently used.

Jaz had taken the precaution of donning Wellies. Townie he might be and the countryside to him was another continent but he had reasoned, "when in the country, do as the country folk do". He ploughed on whilst in the meantime; Pitt surveyed the ground and proceeded as if passing through a minefield. Behind him, Jaz could hear Pitt complaining,

"Damn crap everywhere!"

The farmhouse door was suddenly flung open and a rather menacing figure filled the open doorway; grey hair, weather-beaten face, six feet four and perhaps twenty stones of solid muscle. The man's face gave him the look of an ex-boxer or wrestler whose nose had been punched into an unnatural shape by aggressive opponents.

"You'm trespassin. You lost or something?"

Pitt produced his warrant card and introduced Khunkhun and himself.

Joe Palin rummaged in the top pocket of his grubby plaid shirt and produced a battered pair of spectacles held together with strips of surgical tape. He adjusted them on the bridge of his nose and began to read the card.

"Feckin shotgun licence is it? Well, I can tell you it's right up to date and I'll show you around my secure backroom, then we can all test the 'safe and secure' box I keep it in."

Mumbling something to the effect that coppers were a bloody waste of time, he then without further ado, turned and led the way into the interior. They made their way through the warm heat of a kitchen that smelled of drying clothes, wet dogs, baking and some other noxious odour that Khuhkhun was unable to identify. There was an Aga for cooking and a potbellied wood burner for heat. A huge pile of cut logs was stacked close by. The burner had been turned down low but even that small amount of heat coupled with the remaining heat of the day was sufficient to create a stuffy atmosphere. In the far corner, a couple of sad looking recently snared rabbits hung from heavy metal ceiling hooks and droplets of blood had congealed with the dust on the cracked and discoloured red quarry tiles. The small smeared windows were home to several busy spiders, intent on cocooning flies caught in intricate webs.

A cast iron hand pump supplied water to a battered Belfast sink and Khunkuhn wondered whether all farmhouse kitchens resembled this one. Oh, the joys of isolated country living and how claustrophobic must a snowbound winter be? Cabin fever? No doubt about it he thought. Joe Palin turned his head just in time to catch Pitt's distasteful glance at the dead rabbits.

"Never seen a rabbit waitin ter be skinned 'ave yer?"

Pitt ignored the barb; he hadn't and had never had the least desire to attend a rabbit autopsy. The officers continued on their course through what turned out to be a maze of corridors by way of ascending and descending stairways.

Finally, Palin flicked a light switch and ushered them into a surprisingly comfortable room. There were heavy oak antique dressers and sideboards. These were complemented by deeply buttoned, oxblood coloured leather two and three-seater Chesterfield sofas. There were matching armchairs and an occasional table on which had been placed a vase full of white lilies which gave out an all-pervading fragrance. A drift of petals, some fresh and white some browning at the edges encircled the container. It was Pitt thought a three-dimensional still life oil painting. He stifled a cough as the heady scent caught in his throat. A modern tiled floor was covered with an expensive looking ornate Persian rug. It was the fireplace however that really caught Pitt's eye and without being invited, he bent forward to examine what was undoubtedly no modern copy.

"Genuine Adam. My granddad got it when they demolished the old mansion up the road about seventy years ago. Worth a bloody fortune it is. He always claimed he got it for a hundred Players. Fags were currency during and just after the war. Nice ain't it? Well worth the price I'd say."

Pitt nodded and made himself comfortable in a nearby armchair. Khunkhun followed his colleague's example whilst Joe Palin removed his boots, stripped off his overalls to reveal a sweat shirt and long johns and then lay down on the largest sofa. Pitt sensed it was a gesture of defiance and insolence along the lines of 'You may be the law but you don't impress me much'.

"I'd ask the missus to bring in tea and biscuits on the best china but she's out. Now what's this about my gun licence? It's only been a month since you lot checked the last time. It's a pity you buggers won't leave us farmers alone. After all, it's us and fuckin Geldoff that feed the world."

Pitt replied in a steady unhurried tone,

"It's absolutely nothing to do with your gun licence Mr Palin but everything to do with Tom King and an incident which took place at The Green Man."

Anger boiled over and Palin's face took on an unbridled look of fierceness, livid blue veins and beads of sweat glistening on his forehead. The resulting diatribe was delivered with venom and spittle.

"So he's laid charges 'as he? The bastard! Well I'll tell you; if they 'adn't pulled me off, I'd a made sure he never got into another man's wife's knickers ever again or if he did, he'd a 'ad no tackle to use. Yes, I tried ter do 'im. Pity I didn't 'ave me shotgun with me. Okay, that's it. So what yer goin to do about it eh?"

Pitt waited for a break in the man's harangue and allowed the tension in the room to subside a little.

"So you are telling me that you are unaware that Tom King is dead; murdered?"

Palin sat up, supporting his head with his hands clasped behind his neck. A broad grin lit up his face highlighting the many cracks and ridges the years of outdoor life had created. He was Pitt observed, a very happy farmer indeed.

"Oh please tell me it's true. I 'aven't crossed King's threshold since our little disagreement. He barred me and anyway I've no reason to go to the village. We do our shoppin in Bridgnorth. There's a couple of pints in it for the 'ero that done it though. You've made my day Mr Pitt. Fancy a whisky?"

Pitt declined and Palin grabbed a part empty bottle of Glenmorangie from one of the cupboards and pouring himself a double measure, took a deep slurp and almost purred with contentment. He peered down at the whisky bottle with an expression of adoration in his eyes that only a serious drinker could convey and exclaimed with satisfaction, "Ah lovely stuff."

He proceeded to pour the remaining quarter of a bottle into his glass.

"So where were you last night Mr Palin?"

He replaced the bottle and after a few minutes thought replied,

"It was bit different ter my usual Saturdays. Me and the wife 'ad fed the pigs, and she gathered in the eggs whilst I did a bit of milkin. Usually after that, I'd have a bath and a shave and tart meself up and we'd go into Bridgnorth. Last night though, there were foxes around and I took me gun to 'em. By the time I'd finished, it was too late and anyway I was knackered so we had a night in watchin telly. She'll be back in a minute. She'll bear me out."

Of course she would thought Pitt. Palin sipped his whisky as the door was opened by a petite young woman, pretty and Audrey Hepburn elfin-like. Pitt could just imagine the scene when Palin had found out about her liaison with King. Joe Palin was not the kind of man to take kindly to his possessions being taken and Mrs. Palin gave the impression of delicate porcelain which might easily shatter.

"Here she is. Brenda, meet DCI, is it? Pitt. I've just been explainin that we had a quiet night in last night."

Brenda Palin looked visibly shaken. She blanched and stumbling over her words replied, "Well yes, we err watched TV last night"

The silence in the room was at last broken by Palin. The sneer was whisky induced when he added.

"There you are then Mr. Pitt, just as I said."

Pitt eased himself out of the armchair.

"Right then, we'll leave you to enjoy the rest of your whisky. Perhaps you could both drive over to The Green Man tomorrow? We should have our incident office set up and you can make an official statement. Could you show us a more direct way out please?"

Palin leaned back and opened his mouth before tipping the full glass of whisky, (a quantity sufficient to take down one of his Rottweilers) into his open throat. He paused and replied, "Certainly but there's no way you can avoid wading through pig shit if that was what you'd be thinking."

Pitt sat half in half out of the car, scraping his loafers on an edging stone.

"What do you think guv? "

"There's something going on Jaz but I've no idea what. As far as I'm concerned, it was all too pat."

They had driven half a mile down the track when Pitt called out for Khunkhun to stop and reverse. He pointed a finger towards the lowering sky

"Now isn't that apt? I believe what you see circling that field is what is known as a 'murder' of crows."

Several huge black birds were flocking above them, their 'caws' rang out and echoed across the fields. Now and then, one would break away and swoop down into a dip at the far side of the pasture.

Pitt leapt across the ditch dividing lane from the field and parting the scrub at the edge of the grassland, made his way in the direction of the birds. Khunkhun had by now switched off the ignition and was following him. Reaching the top of the incline, they were able to see what was causing the creatures to gather.

Khunkhun was reminded of nature programs on the TV where the carcass of some unfortunate antelope had been left for scavenging vultures to pick clean. Perhaps a dozen black crows flapped their wings and tore with bloody beaks at something large lying in the dip below them.

Several looked up from their feasting, their malevolent yellow eyes surveying the human intruders. The metallic sweet smell of recent death coupled with the acidic odour of bird droppings filled the air as the officers neared.

"Right Jaz, time to race me down the hill, whilst at the same time flapping your arms as if you are about to take off and swearing as loudly as you can. Ready, steady.........go!"

They dashed in tandem towards the feeding birds, shouting loudly. The crows arose as one, skimming over their heads, screaming out defiant ugly squawks as they headed for safety. Soon only one remained, strutting up and down upon the prone heap, every now and then pecking at some tasty morsel of flesh. Pitt kicked out at the bird which, after retrieving one last beak full, made an unsteady wobbling takeoff and disappeared amongst the others now wheeling far above, ready to jostle for positions once these meddling humans had retreated. Bloated bluebottles hovered and buzzed above the carcass. Pitt suspected the eggs had been laid and that any time now the offspring would be wriggling their way to the surface. It would be found, overblown with internal gasses and the constant movement of writhing maggots deep within giving the impression of the return of life to the remains. Pitt had often witnessed the putrefaction of corpses. What had lived and which once had a personality, had loved or hated and had the ability to think and make decisions was now left to the mercy of rampant bacteria.

"It's poor old Brock the Badger Jaz and oh what have we here? I think we can assume this was no suicide or the result of old age. It seems that someone has decided that it's time for an early badger cull and if I was a betting man, I'd stake my house on guessing who's responsible. No wonder Palin's wife was edgy. She thought we were there to discuss this chap. If we'd taken a look at Palin's shotgun, you can bet that we'd have found residue showing it had been fired recently. Of course, he'd say he'd shot rats. There is no way so I'm told that shotgun pellets can be pinned down to a particular gun. A load of buckshot cannot be traced to a weapon but should Palin have been stupid enough to leave the shell casing then a match would be possible but I don't believe he is stupid; far from it. Furthermore, going out at night to take pot shots at the local wildlife does not rule him out as a suspect for King's murder. If Mrs Palin is as terrified of him as she seems, she would not only lie regarding the minor offence of shooting badgers but would provide an alibi for a more serious offence."

Chapter 12

"Want the good news or the weird news guv?"

Pitt had been examining a string of fat that he was stripping from a slice of bacon in his sandwich. He flicked it into the waste bin by his desk and licked away the brown sauce staining his fingers.

"Time was Jaz when the bacon was grilled to perfection in the canteen. Falling standards everywhere. I'll take the good news."

He wrapped the sandwich in a paper napkin and took a deep gulp of black coffee from the Styrofoam beaker.

"We've got a DNA match from the handle of the mallet. Turns out that when Bella's young knight in shining tattoos got into that bit of bother, the local Force took fingerprints and DNA for their records. Some argument about 'The Wolves', apparently, he's a fan of the team. Not everyone is it seems. He lays one on this guy; the lad's mates join in and it turns into a John Wayne bar-room brawl. The local coppers told me that there were glasses, chairs and tables everywhere plus a few broken windows. The only thing missing was the honky-tonk piano and the buxom, caring tart. Anyway, he gets a fine, has to pay for the damage and gets sent to the Young Offenders Institution at Brynsford for a month or two."

Pitt was pleased and took another bite from his butty, swallowed, and swilled it down with coffee.

"Well, if you add to that Dean's adoration of the fragrant Bella together with her recent bruises, we have a motive. Time to wheel him in Jaz. Great work by the way."

Khunkhun indicated a note of caution.

"Well not so fast guv. This is where it gets weird. Turns out Young Lochinvar is one of a matching pair of twins."

"So what Jaz, the DNA would still be unique."

"But not if you're talking Siamese twins. Take a look at this."

Khunkhun passed a copy of a local newspaper of two or more decades earlier. The monochrome photo showed babies cuddling each other. The caption read; 'Shropshire lady in double joy.' The article explained that the pair were conjoined twins who, because they were joined at the leg would require a comparatively simple operation to separate. As no vital organs were shared, the babies would go on to lead perfectly normal lives.

"I've talked it over with 'He who knows all' guv. Bryn told me that, and I quote;

'The egg is fertilised by a single sperm which splits into two embryos resulting in two foetuses with identical DNA.'"

"Unfortunately, that seems pretty clear Jaz and perfectly logical."

"It gets worse. Dean was behind the bar that afternoon and the place was absolutely heaving. He has hundreds of punters who would back up his alibi. Okay, there are calls of nature that could be extended to include a quick hammer job but as we saw, the whole setup in the brewery was meticulously presented like some stage set. It would have taken considerable time to arrange the scene. Furthermore, in addition to the undressing, etc. he needed to make his way into a room which it was known, Tom King would have locked and which was still locked later. There's the possibility he had a spare key of course but the door was bolted on the inside and in any case, it's the time element that tends to rule him out. "

"Do we have any information about his twin brother on that day? There's always that possibility that they might have swapped places at the bar. If the place was so crowded, that could have been done without the other bar staff or Bella noticing anything different."

"He's a local lad, farm labourer and wait for it, sometimes he also gives a hand with the brewing and therefore you might expect to find his DNA on the handle.

I guess that working up there; he would have some idea regarding locking doors but even so...............You have a situation where the DNA would be the same and both have some knowledge of the brewery."

Pitt picked up the remains of his sandwich, looked at it, then tossed it into the bin.

"Well thanks for that Jaz. Now would you like to bugger off and come back with good tidings of great joy for me? Perhaps something a little more palatable than that bacon butty?

Khunkhun clicked his heels and winked as he gave a salute before smartly marching out of Pitt's office.

Pitt smiled.

"Cheeky young bugger."

Chapter 13

Pitt had ensured that the mundane but vitally important routine police work was in train and the portable H.Q. was buzzing with activity. The list which Bella King had provided was being worked through and statements were taken. It was time for Pitt to spend time with the locals in the bar of The Green Man.

He had always been able to mingle, buying a pint or two. Then as long as he didn't 'come the copper', he had found that people would usually open up. In many cases, there was a correlation between pints bought and information gained. Talk of the Raggy Men brought forth much nudge-nudge, wink-winking from the older drinkers in particular. Pitt began to form a picture from what was said that these men not only banged sticks together but that some were in fact business partners. Indeed, it seemed that the dancers had formed a company and bought up land in the area. Some had already owned land and the extent of shares allocated reflected either cash or land brought into the company.

The general consensus was that most of the land owned was unsuitable for farming and when he asked why anyone would gather a portfolio of worthless land, the old chap who had so far cost him five pints of Guinness began to open up. In a voice cracking with the resonance of dry leaves he began.

"Bloody obvious init! Thought you was a detective. They wanna build an estate; bloody affordable homes and all that stuff, 'ousing for the peasants. Hovels more like at fancy prices. Mek a bloody fortune they will."

His Adam's apple bobbed in and out of a shirt collar that once might have fitted his neck but was now far too large. Pitt was reminded of Galapagos tortoises as they craned ancient necks out of their shells. Khunkhun arrived from the bar holding yet another pint of Guinness. Pitt slid the fresh pint across the table to the man and asked,

"So when are they going to start the development then?"

The ancient face, skin rutted and grey like elephant hide broke into a smirk. The dewdrop on the end of his nose would drop any minute now Pitt thought.

"They aint, they can't cos they aint got no access to the Bridgnorth Road. No bloody builder's goin ter build 'ouses you'd need an 'elecopter ter get outa."

Pitt frowned.

"So why would they invest in a project like that then. Surely there must be a way through?"

"Cause they thought yer jed man Tom King would flog off a piece of 'is land. If yer look at the bit at the side of the pub, it leads right down ter the main road. Perfect access; opens up loads a land."

"And he wouldn't sell to them?"

"Oh are 'e'd sell all right but 'ard nosed bastard that he was, he wanted a bloody fortune for it. If 'eed a got it, they'd a made sod all out the deal. Just shows 'ow confident they was. They bought up the end terrace house. There's the pub, then there's number one, number two, number three Green Man Villas. Then there's number four, all boarded up. That's the one they bought. King's land is next to it and they'd a demolished it, made good the gable end and got themselves a nice wide road when King's land was added."

"So there was no chance of King selling and without his land, their investment was worthless?"

"Din't matter to 'im, he was mekin a good livin outa the pub.'E just 'ad ter wait,'old out and wait till they cum a beggin. Is missus is part owner and er'd a sold out but they'm partners see and it needed 'em both ter sign. 'Er's a good sort 'er is and I reckon it'll go through now. You cum back in a year er two and you'll see fifty bloody monstrosities built full a young folk and their snotty-nosed kids. Hope I'm not around. Any chance of another pint?"

He wiped the dribble of froth from his upper lip and pointed a raw-boned hand to his empty glass. Pitt smiled and indicated to Khunkhun that more Guinness was in order.

Chapter14

The weather was fine, the boss was back in Wolverhampton and Jaz looked forward to the bottle of water plus apple, orange and yogurt he'd brought with him for lunch. Today the usual bruised banana he carried had been dispensed with. He'd have a quick snack and then it would be back to endless interviews with men who as far as he was concerned, danced silly dances.

Where might he go to clear his mind, find half an hour's peace and relax? Jaz eyed the pointed steeple of St Egbert's church. The silver cross at the pinnacle shone brightly. Perhaps there might be a bench where he could sit and think. A brass plate on the stone wall explained that the church had taken its name from the Anglo-Saxon holy man who legend had it had escaped from the invading Vikings. The man had been whisked up to Heaven still attached to a wooden cross after being tossed into the Severn in readiness for a little Viking target practice. From Khunkhun's knowledge of history, being caught by these marauders or perhaps losing a battle would usually result in very unpleasant things coming your way.

Jaz smiled to himself. He could imagine Bryn Edwards doing the autopsy on some Dark Ages king and Pitt having to read his report. "In my opinion Pitt, the man was already dead after his whipping and as you can see, one of the twenty arrows had pierced his heart. The beheading was incidental."

The gentle warmth of the day, the blue sky and stillness created a kind of sensation which Jaz had experienced many times before in such places. Crickets chirruped and pigeons called to each other but that did not disturb the feeling of tranquillity. There was indeed a bench made of varnished light wood which bore the inscription in memory of a loving wife and mother. Jaz sat, gulped down a mouthful of Perrier water, took out an apple from his pocket and rubbed it on his trousers. He was about to take a bite when he became aware of a mechanical whirring sound and looking up, he could see a man in a motorised wheelchair navigating his way with some difficulty through the lych gate. The man stretched an arm, pushed open the gates and came bumping along on the cobbles. As he approached, he gave a perfunctory wave and wheezed out, "Lovely day for it."

Jaz nodded an acknowledgement. He could see a large bunch of daffodils, trumpets standing out yellow against the black of the man's jeans and tee shirt. At first he was a little irked at having his free time disturbed. It then occurred to him that this might be the dancer yet to be interviewed. From the reports he had seen, there was one disabled Raggy Man in the group. He doubted that the man would add much to the information received as it had been stated that he had left the proceedings shortly after the completion of his allotted dances and had not joined his friends in The Green Man. Still, boxes had to be ticked; witness statements had to be signed.

He could see the man's rear as his chair made its wobbling journey down the pathway. He was now some fifty yards distant. Jaz cupped his hands to his mouth and bellowed,

"Hello! Are you one of the Raggy Men?"

At first, it seemed that the disabled man had not heard him but just as Jaz was repeating his call, the wheelchair was manoeuvred into a half turn and the man replied,

"Yes, but who are you? I never speak to the Press if that's who you are."

Khunkhun tossed his half-eaten apple into the litter bin at the side of the bench and jogged towards the wheelchair.

"There's many who are of the same mind with regard to the Press sir. Actually, I'm one of the investigating officers into Tom King's murder at The Green Man and we haven't had you down at the police cabin for an interview."

"It's a bit difficult at the moment. I've a little ceremony to perform."

"That's okay I'll not interfere. I'm DS Khunkhun .and if my memory serves me, you would be Stan Till? Perhaps we could chat as you go about your business?"

The man eyed him suspiciously then after a brief pause answered,

"Yes okay, you could probably give me a hand anyway. I s'pose as you can see, I've got plenty of time. No great hurry in my case. Copped this in Helmand. Shrapnel you know. It can hurt like hell at times but hey, all in the line of duty for Queen and Country or that's what they tell me. The pension's not too bad; pays for the fags and beer anyway. To think, I was once a sergeant and now I'm a bloody useless cripple. To look at me now, you wouldn't believe I was once the Brigade's swimming champion. Hell I once did a sponsored Channel swim. Now that was one mother of an experience. Jellyfish stings all over. Still it raised a few grand for The British Legion so it was worth it."

There was bitterness coming through Khunkhun thought but then who wouldn't be bitter in his predicament. One day you're a fit leader of men, next you're reliant on the battery in your wheelchair not going flat. He brought the conversation back to the events at The Green Man.

"I believe you left early once the dancing was over?"

Till smiled ruefully.

"Grown men dancing around wearing rags is odd and it's even stranger when they do it wearing a mask with a face sprouting leaves. Yes, you're correct, I left the party before it started. They can be a bit boring you know but their hearts are in the right place. Found a spot for me didn't they; a bloke who can't dance 'cause he's in a wheelchair joining a dance group. I've lived here all my life. The family used to rent one of the cottages in the old terrace; The Green Man Villas, so when I finished my career, I bought a rundown place and had it done up, well the main bit anyway; couldn't afford to do the lot. It's just a little out of the village, wanted a bit of peace and quiet; needed to reflect and plan the rest of what was left of my life. Never thought I'd end up a bloody Morris Dancer. Good job none of my army mates live around here! Some visit me but I don't crack on about the group. They really would take the piss, wouldn't they? Still, the way I look at it is that it's all harmless fun and to have a go at the dancers is a bit like kicking one of those nice friendly golden Labradors. You just don't do things like that do you?"

Stan Till chuckled to himself and asked, "Want ter see where The Green Man is supposedly buried or should I say reinterred? Legend has it that they dug him up, doused him in holy water and stuck him as close as they could to the church wall. It's all my eye and Betty Martin really. From what I've read, some say The Green Man's an emissary of goodness, rebirth, that kind of thing. Surely that's the same as the Christian resurrection?"

He looked Jaz full in the face and smiled.

"Still, that's not your faith I guess?"

"Maybe not. Sikh by birth and as you might say, agnostic by nature. Yes, I do know a bit about the bible; Religious Studies O' Level passed with flying colours."

Till shrugged.

"Good for you then. What was your name again? Come on I'll show you, it's on the way to where my sister's buried."

Jaz provided the man with his abbreviated name and followed his bumpy progress down towards the far side of the graveyard. Recent shiny marble slabs gave way to crumbling lichen encrusted stones. The damage was such that it would have been impossible to read names, dates, or tributes. Little had been done to cut back encroaching vegetation and in many cases briars and ivy had totally covered graves. At times, self-setting saplings sprouted

63

from long abandoned tombs. Then to Khunkhun's surprise, they entered into yet another area of recent interments.

"When they planted him out here all those years ago, they hadn't the foresight to realise that at some future time they would need to use this area. That's him there, let's hope there's no need to move him a second time."

Close to the wall, untended and handed back to nature was a small plot. The contrast with that and other graves was stark indeed. Khunkhun picked up a branch blown into the cemetery and poked about on the grave. After a while, he could just make out etched on the stone, a grotesque head, almost hidden by carvings of leaves and branches giving a macabre unworldly look to what purported to be a human skull. Beneath this, he could make out the word 'Resurgam'.

"How very nice but why the Latin? Surely that means 'I shall rise again' or something similar? Why would they want this ugly looking bloke to return?"

"Well from what I've read, and don't get the idea I'm some kind of 'anorak', it's just that being so close to the grave I tend, it interested me. The theory is that a new form, a new body will arise, casting off his woody bits. He'd once more be a man, complete and perfect, a bit like Christ rising on the third day all shining and new so to speak. By the looks of it that bit must have been chiselled on at a later date when ideas about The Green Man had changed and rather than being fearful of his return, they looked upon it as bringing good times around here."

There was a pause in the conversation. Stan Till gazed fixedly into the distance at the patchwork of rolling fields which looked very much like a painting by Constable. Somewhere far off, smoke was curling up into the blue. Khunknun spoke quietly.

"And your sister's grave is close by?"

Till turned and seemed to mentally shake himself back into the present.

"Oh, she's just over there. Alice was only seventeen and I was away then. I couldn't even get back for the funeral and as both of my parents are dead, I had to rely on relatives. The army gave me compassionate leave but by the time I'd got back from the front line and managed to hitch a ride with the RAF, it was too late. It's been on my conscience ever since but I guess if you're surrounded by a bunch of rag 'eads, (whoops sorry officer, shouldn't say that; political correctness and that sort of thing) it's tricky trying to get back to the UK. Anyway, I try to visit her as often as I can with a bunch of flowers. She loved flowers. I once read that Eskimos have forty or fifty words for snow. I guess at the time I could have matched that in words for grief."

His voice trailed away. Jaz averted his gaze; not wishing to embarrass a war hero when he was shedding a tear. Stan Till pressed buttons, turned knobs on his machine then moved slowly forward towards the grave. On stopping, he lent forward, removed the wilting flowers which had been left by him previously and gently placed two bunches of daffodils on the gleaming marble slab. It was a simple yet moving act after which they silently nodded to each other before going their separate ways.

Chapter 15

"Interesting stuff, company documentation guv."

"Well, I s'pose with your recent academic life and all it might just be your kind of thing. I can just see you curled up in front of a blazing log fire, glass of malt whisky in hand and thumbing through a company prospectus."

"Can't say I'd go that far guv but the Memorandum and Articles of Association can be worth their weight in gold. I now know who owns Raggy Investments Ltd for instance."

"For God's sake Jaz, they surely didn't incorporate 'Raggy' in the company name?"

'Fraid so and the ownership is quite surprising. The major shareholders are quite interesting. We find that fifteen percent of the shares are owned by Bella King and twenty percent by a Peter Jackman. He paid seventy-five thousand for his investment. There are four other minor shareholders all of whom are members of The Raggy Men. Most made over tranches of land at valuations equivalent to pay for their shareholdings. Tom King of course owns the majority of shares in Raggy Investments."

"Mmm, perhaps the sharp as a needle Bella King might have worked out that it might be financially worthwhile to push hubby into the fermentation tank. She would then be in possession of his share of what is by all accounts a very valuable public house in its own right. More importantly, she would be in a position to negotiate a deal with the developers which would be more acceptable to them. Bella would be a very rich widow indeed."

"Taking it a step further sir, this might make our theories about Dean Jones firm up. What if it's true that Mrs King has got a thing going with young Dean? He's not the sharpest knife in the drawer and if she were to drop out to him how nice it would be if only she were free of

King and having plenty of money........... Maybe he'd been thinking about it for months and then, bang! She appears in the bar obviously having been at the wrong end of King's anger."

Khunkhun smirked and thrust out his chest, very pleased with his explanation.

"And I guess you're going to tell me how the not too bright Jones brothers managed to get into a room locked on the inside?"

"Well as it happens, I think I may have come up with an idea on that one as well guv."

"Okay Jaz, give."

Chapter 16

"So it's your theory that the brewery can be accessed via the cottages? I tell you Jaz, I just hope this creeping around in the middle of the night is going to be of some use."

They carefully picked their way through the entanglement of briars, shrubs and long since abandoned lawn which now sprouted a rich array of dandelions. Now and then they mumbled the odd expletive as waving briar thorn scraped their faces or a nettle brushed their hands. Each had a heavy-duty flashlight and Pitt had brought along a crowbar. The light would be used sparingly once they were within but for now, they relied on the sporadic silver moonlight for illumination.

Pitt had joked as he extracted the bar from his car boot.

"Be prepared for anything Jaz. Us boy scouts are ready for all emergencies."

Dusk had long since completed its shift and had handed over to a starry barmy evening as they approached the back door of the end-terraced cottage. The once creamy white pebble dash had morphed into a dirty shade of grey and in places, the ingress of damp had produced a black mould.

The appearance of dereliction was completed by every window and doorway being protected by sheets of what had originally been half-inch thick plywood screwed into window and door frames. Slimy green layers had accumulated on many of the protective covers and the elements had caused edges to split or bend. Nevertheless, the original screws still kept the plywood in position.

Pitt glanced across at the adjoining cottage. All was quiet and only the quivering white light from a television evidenced any habitation. A Russian vine had made steady progress across the lawn and was now waving its many tendrils in the direction of the neighbouring garden. From deep within the greenery, a long-abandoned group of weathered gnomes were trying bravely to give the intruders a welcoming smile.

Pitt whispered through cupped hands," Jaz, I reckon we're about to enter the home of the neighbours from hell."

"No expense spared guv, literally no expense. You sure we're okay breaking in like this?"

"We're cops Jaz, here to maintain H. M's peace and I am sure I heard noises in this property. We must therefore do our duty and investigate."

Khunkhun signalled a thumbs up and grinned.

"Yes, I think I can hear it now sir, better get in as soon as possible."

Lights were switched on in a couple of rooms next door and just as suddenly curtains were drawn so that now only spears of orange glow lit up the adjacent garden. No light pierced the unwelcoming gloom which enveloped the end terrace. They stumbled towards the back door to be greeted by loud hissing and two evil-looking orbs. They approached cautiously and were confronted by a huge black cat that seemed to have taken over the role of doorkeeper.

"That's one nasty bugger of a cat Jaz. Pure evil!"

Pitt whispered. He had never been a cat person

"Mmm my Uncle Dagle loves cats guv.

"P'raps you could see what he makes of this one then Jaz?"

Pitt moved forward and gently eased the cat from the step with his foot. He was met with further hissing, rows of sharp teeth and vicious looking claws but after this initial show of disdain and arching of the back, it lumbered away in the direction of the front gate.

In the blackness, Pitt's hands moved carefully along the edge of the wooden covering feeling for any weak spot. At last, he found what he was expecting. At a point halfway up the doorway, the wood had been wrenched away and then hurriedly screwed back in position. The same was true at both the top and bottom. Someone had thought it worthwhile to break into the property and by the look of the fresh-looking wooden splinters lying on the doorstep, this had been done recently.

Pitt slipped the tapered end of the wrench into a small gap between the door frame and the ply and tried to lever off the covering. Progress was slow and Pitt moved the tool up and down as areas split under the pressure he exerted.

"Damn! They've used wood screws instead of nails Jaz. This might take longer than we had planned."

Eventually, the final screw was levered from its hold and Jaz steadied the plywood before the two officers lowered it to the floor. The door was now revealed and a cursory glance showed that the lock had been forced. Pitt turned the knob and gently pushed. Grit and debris had been trapped beneath the door and there was a scraping sound as it was gradually forced ajar.

Once across the threshold they switched on their flashlights, aiming the glare in the direction of the floor so that only a small area was illuminated at any one time. From a far corner, they heard a squeaking chattering sound. This was followed shortly afterwards by a scratching and a rustling. Khunkhun took a step back towards the door.

"Bloody rats! I bloody hate rats. My uncle had 'em in his shop years ago when I was a kid. Used to go around with machete smashing the buggers' heads. Even so, in the end, he had to call in the rat-man. Place was alive with 'em."

Pitt gave his subordinate a paternal pat on the shoulder.

"Remind me never to buy anything edible from your uncle's shop Jaz. Have no fear my boy. Should any come within biting distance I shall despatch Mr. Rattus Rattus as we Latin scholars call him with one blow from my trusty torch."

Pitt's wry smile disguised a truth that he had always thought that a heavy-duty metal torch was a very useful weapon in his world where villains would have no compunction to use a knife should they be cornered and where police carried nightsticks of limited use. Of course, one might tazer a perp but then there would be the inevitable form filling and cross-examination by one's seniors and of course, there was always the possibility of accidentally killing some scrote who suffered from a dodgy heart. Yes, the torch was his weapon of choice, and well, after all, it was a perfectly innocent tool that was very easy to explain away in the event of being asked in cross-examination by some highly-paid barrister to explain his actions. No barrister of any worth would believe the account to be the truth but then how could they rebut the assertion?

"He came at me. The only thing I had to protect myself was the torch, sir. What could I do under the circumstances?"

Pitt led the way towards the stairs through the jumble of broken chairs and an upturned table. He played the beam across the room finally allowing it to arrow towards an area at the foot of the stairs. Clearly visible in the thick layer of dust were the recent imprints of shoes. Pitt motioned towards them and whispered;

"Careful not to disturb them."

They sidled up the stairs, backs against the wall until they reached the landing. The tracks were still clearly evident. They ended a few yards in and Pitt circled the beam until it shone onto a substantial looking hall table, cabriole legs and stained dark oak. By the looks of it, this had been dragged across the landing and positioned beneath what Pitt believed was a trap door leading into the loft area.

"Looks as though you were absolutely correct Jaz. Give me a hand."

Pitt clambered onto the table and wrenched himself up to his full height. The flap was small but sufficient for a normal sized man or woman to squeeze through. He pushed at the trapdoor. It opened and fell back upon the floorboards within the loft area.

"Careful guv, you'll wake the dead!"

"Maybe Jaz, we're certainly close enough to the graveyard, eh? Pass me the torch will you?"

He hoisted himself through the aperture with difficulty but finally managed to pull himself free and sit, feet dangling above the landing. He let out a triumphant,

"Yes!"

He had directed the beam towards the adjoining property. The hole was just large enough to crawl through into the neighbour's loft. Pitt scrabbled his way across to the entrance and shone the powerful beam horizontally through the gap. He could just make out similar openings in the walls of other cottages within the terrace. The answer to the riddle of how King's murderer had entered and exited a locked brewery was obvious. All that was needed was to return to The Green Man and locate the loft cover.

Time to leave the cottage now. The officers closed the door and reattached the plywood onto the still protruding screw fixings, placing a couple of boulders against the board. Then having checked that the property looked secure, they made their way back along the path, out across the village green and up the hill to the vicarage. The unmarked police car had been parked on the roughed out hard standing of slate chippings which served as a parking area for worshippers. There were no signs of activity from within the parsonage. Khunkhun released the hand brake and allowed the car to roll down the hill. It was only when they were clear of the village that he brought the car into motion and headed towards Bridgnorth.

Pitt was aware that it would be necessary to give a reason for the SOCOs to enter the property and do their work. Also, though they had been careful not to leave fingerprints by using their nitrile gloves, nevertheless, it was quite possible that in the semi-darkness of the cottage, there could well be evidence of their illegal entry that they had missed. Therefore, the following day, he would make a great show of calling in on all of the cottages in the row and asking whether they had been aware of any suspicious noises within the end terrace. There was always someone who would be apprehensive about a derelict occupancy and mostly this was well justified. This would give Pitt the excuse to re-enter and call in the specialists.

Chapter 17

"I've had our lads check out the builders employed on the reroofing boss. The gaffer in charge was extremely helpful after we suggested we might make a call to the tax office. In fact, he did it all on the cheap and there were only three of them involved. He did the bulk of the work himself helped by a Paddy who went back to Ireland once the job was done and guess who was the third man?"

Shades of Orson Wells in 'The third man' thought Pitt.

"Is this some kind of quiz game Jaz? Just get on with it will you!"

Khunkhun pulled up an office chair and then adopting an expression way beyond smug he began;

"The locals told me that when King, err out of the goodness of his heart, paid most of the bill for reroofing the terrace, he had a local company do the job; cash in hand; no VAT; no Income Tax for the builder. Okay so far, just what you'd expect from King. Also he'd tell the householders they'd got a brilliant deal and from what we saw when we made our house calls most are getting on a bit and would think the sun shone out of King's anus. The thing is though that Dean Jones's twin was between farming jobs at the time. He'd often do a bit of labouring for this builder and this was a steady six months of roofing work. I'm told he's got far more muscle than brain and hod carrying up and down ladders is what's required to get the tiles up to the roofer. "

"So what you're thinking Jaz is that the brothers might have planned a project which would top up their finances?"

"That's how I see it but circumstances might have resulted in a change of plan. As we know, friend Dean has been involved in a bit of GBH and from what I've heard from the locals, the other brother, Andy is a dab hand with snares and supplies a butcher in Bridgnorth with rabbits or a brace or two of pheasants. Crawling through lofts and into premises which they have previously sussed out might also be quite lucrative. By the looks of some of the knickknacks on show in the cottages, there are a few valuable antiques to be fenced, not to mention the possibility of a few thousand in notes under the mattress. Maybe this might have taken its natural course but for young Deano's ardour and his anger at seeing his hoped-for lady friend getting slapped about by Tom King. Could be also that he's so taken in by Mrs. King that once the King is dead and the cry goes up "Long live the Queen!" he thinks he'll become the consort or even the new king. Farfetched I'd say but the lad's none too bright, is he? Maybe she might have encouraged him. It's not beyond the realms of possibility, is it? Remember she's now a very wealthy woman."

"Great job Jaz, I think it's time for another chat with our Madam King and this time we'll make it under caution and give her the opportunity to take legal advice then we'll see what the Siamese twins have to say."

Chapter 18

The officers sat in a back area of the Portacabin which had been erected to the side of The Green Man. All recording devices had been checked. Though privacy was of the essence, Pitt had opened the sliding windows and then pulled down the blinds. It was one of those rare hot almost windless late spring days. The cabin was close enough to the pub for there to be an occasional gentle waft of last night's beer mingled with the smell of stale cigarettes emanating from the outside smoking shelter.

Mrs. King made one of her dramatic entrances, posing for a moment in The Green Man's doorway looking for all the world as if she was involved in a fashion shoot. Then, giving a coquettish wave in the direction of the Portacabin and swaying on six-inch high 'killer' heels, red suede, ankle straps and not quite Jimmy Choo, she slowly walked towards the wooden steps leading into the temporary police station.

Pitt was aware of the clacking of shoes as Bella King entered engulfed in a cloud of expensive perfume. Pitt noted that the sweater was tight but not tarty; the same applied to the black skirt which ended just above the knee and gave the viewer a glimpse of shapely thighs. The lady was carefully made up Pitt surmised in a way that complimented her daytime image. The evening image he had noticed was more heavily emphasized. Well, pub lighting and her evening incarnation behind the bar was he thought necessary in order to please the punters and they certainly got their money's worth from Mrs. King. Pitt had always been aware of his weakness for good-looking, intelligent women, and this one had a decent degree from a good university. He must therefore attempt to keep Bella King at arm's length in this investigation. Good-looking, intelligent women were just as capable of heinous crimes as dowdy, frumpish, and stupid females, possibly more so he thought.

"Come in Mrs King, take a seat."

"Please use my first name. Bella."

She sighed languorously and added,

"Thank you, inspector, but as we have met previously, perhaps we can dispense with formality? Such a lovely day don't you think?"

She smiled a brilliant smile and cupped her chin under her right hand, elbow on the table, a perfect photographic pose. Pitt averted his eyes and smoothed out a checklist he had previously prepared.

"Certain things have come to light during the course of our investigation and we would like to hear your take on these. I shall have to caution you so if you wish to postpone our meeting or rearrange to meet in Wolverhampton that will be up to you and of course you may have your solicitor present."

Mrs King showed no signs of discomfort, surveyed her perfectly manicured blood red varnished nails and after a moment replied,

"Ben, may I call you Ben? I will go along with what you advise."

Pitt was determined to return the conversation to a formal basis.

"I'm sorry Mrs King but I cannot be seen to influence you in your decision but I will say that you will undoubtedly find my questioning intrusive. I make no apologies for that. This is a murder case and I shall ask whatever is necessary to get to the truth of the matter."

Bella King frowned, feigned an air of indecisiveness and replied in a slightly hardened tone.

"Breeze on then Inspector, I'm yours for the next hour or so but then I'll have to check out the bar before we open. I don't need a solicitor as I have nothing to hide so if that is okay with you, please proceed with the light in the face and the rubber hammer."

Pit smiled. "Sorry I can't accommodate you on that one. We just don't do that anymore."

She gave a little flick of her head and a curl fell across her face.

"Right, I believe you are a major shareholder in the rather strangely named 'Raggy Investments Ltd.'? Am I correct?"

Pitt was aware of the constant movement of her arms and hands either denoting passion or lack of interest dependent on what was required. This time it was a flicking away of some imaginary fly from above her head and a casual;

"You're very sharp this morning Inspector. Well as you have obviously gone through the documentation with a fine-toothed comb, the answer is 'Yes'. I have no idea why you would ask."

"Sharp yes Mrs. King but to put it bluntly, this would create a conflict of interest between your husband and yourself regarding the sale of land to the side of The Green Man?"

"Once more Inspector, it's a case of 'No shit Sherlock!'. Quite obviously the answer to that is also 'Yes'. We argued a great deal about this particular matter and I guess that by now your investigative nose would have smelt a rat regarding my story of a fall down stairs. Tom was a very aggressive man if you crossed him as many around here will tell you. Sorry about that, cuff me guv, it's a fair cop, I lied. To be serious, I found it very embarrassing to admit that my husband was a wife-beater."

Pitt offered a wry smile as he said,

"On this occasion, I shan't be warming up a cell for you but I do advise you that it's best to be frank with me. Be under no illusions that if you withhold evidence from my investigation, I shall have no compunction about charging you."

Bella King was in no way cowed.

"Mmm honesty being the best policy and all that stuff? Anyway, I wanted to sell but he, greedy bastard that he always was held out for a great deal more. In time, I guess the company would have received a compromise figure somewhere between the original (which I thought reasonable) offer and his mega figure."

"You would then have gone on and made a considerable sum from the sale of the unlocked land?"

"Yep, that's about the strength of it. I didn't need to use my Ph.D. in Business Studies to work that out."

She had obviously slipped her degree into the conversation to impress and Pitt was indeed impressed. Once more; beautiful and intelligent, in his eyes a potent combination.

"Was there any timescale for the project?"

"No not really and in fact, the value would have increased. Should you have cause to look in the estate agents' windows in Bridgnorth, you will see that prices in this area move north at a much faster rate than elsewhere in Shropshire. No, I'm in no hurry personally. I can't speak for other investors though as I am not aware of their circumstances. I do know that most were for their own reasons, very unhappy about my husband's attitude."

Pitt doubted the truth of her answer. Bella King he was sure knew exactly what shape the finances of other shareholders were in. He said,

"I suppose though that it would mean that you could afford a complete break with a man who was at times rather brutal Mrs King?"

"I guess you're implying that I might have had enough cash to make an over-the-top offer for Tom's share of The Green Man or start up elsewhere? Actually, I love the place and yes, it's true I would have stumped up plenty of cash to have it all to myself. Things have gone remarkably well over the past few years. Pity I hadn't the wherewithal when we started the venture and had to rely on Tom coming up with the money. That may seem obvious to you but I knew Tom well enough to understand that he would never have sold out. Apart from the fact that he also loved the pub and I have to admit, he was good at what he did. He would never have sold just to spite me as well as maintain his hold over me. 'Never have sold out'. Oh dear, have I just made myself a suspect again?"

Yes, you have and it's probably a double bluff thought Pitt. He continued.

"But now he's dead, I guess that problem is solved, Mrs King?"

"I didn't kill my husband. I might have felt like it but I'm a coward in that department. I even have a thing about killing spiders and I really feckin hate those."

"Yes, I do see that but would there be anyone who'd take it upon themselves to act as your proxy?"

"Ah, a case of 'Murder in the Cathedral' you think Inspector? 'Who will rid me of this meddlesome priest?' Sorry Inspector, I'm no Henry the Second and I can guarantee Tom was no Thomas a Becket. Tom always struck first you see. You suspect young toy boy with his record of violence might come to my aid? Well you're wrong there. He's kept a clean sheet over the years in spite of constant provocation from my husband. Furthermore, I've made it quite clear to him that whilst It's fine to escort any troublemaker to the door, excessive force, which I have to say he's quite capable of would result in a P45 in double-quick time. Now unless you have any more probing questions on your checklist, I'd like to open up."

She stood, smoothed her skirt with both hands and moved, with a kind of feline litheness towards the door. She did not look back. The weather had changed and gusts of cooling wind twirled crisp packets and discarded cigarette cartons as Mrs King clasped her arms folded across her chest. Pitt watched as she disappeared into the inner darkness.

"I am certain we shall be interviewing that lady again very shortly Jaz. There's plenty that she still hasn't told us and we shall dig as deep as is needed to find what that might be."

Khunkhun smiled and asked with an air of mock innocence, "You mean you don't think she's telling the truth guv?"

Pitt turned to his subordinate with a knowing look before walking away.

Chapter 19

"We need to see them both Jaz. I know it's a bit Hitchcock and fairly obvious but it's not unknown for identical twins to provide alibis for each other"

The following day, Pitt led Dean Jones down the steps and into interview room 12a whilst Khunkhun sat opposite his brother Andy in the adjoining room 12b. The rooms had been selected to provide a swift means of communication between the officers should that be required.

The usual formalities were observed and both brothers declined the offer of a solicitor. Pitt suspected that this was all part of the macho image. We can deal with these 'pigs' without the help of some upper-class suit to plead our case. Pitt commenced the interview;

"I think you know why you are here Mr Jones. In view of your past record, your obvious regard for Mrs King; your dislike for Mr. King and your knowledge of the brewery, we have every reason to question you regarding Tom King's murder."

Jones said nothing, rubbed a finger over what Pitt assumed was a recent addition to his tattoo picture gallery and looked Pitt straight in the face. The latter glanced down at the man's arm. The newly arrived artwork was a red heart pierced by an arrow and the word 'Love' etched below in blue. Pitt had no great knowledge of 'tatts' but he thought the design might be a little passé in this day and age. He sat back and waited for a response.

"So wadja want ter know then?"

"Well for starters, I'd like to know how much you and your brother discussed the renovation work undertaken on the cottages in The Green Man Terrace."

Jones's attitude was sneering.

"Why would I be interested in roofing? I'm head barman and assistant brewer. I don't need that shit."

"Yes we are well aware of your day job and Mrs. King has given you a sparkling reference regarding your work. What we are interested in is your extra-curricular activities Mr Jones and I don't mean having a game of five aside. It's rumoured and I emphasize only rumoured that you and your brother have indulged in a little housebreaking to augment your main source of income. I'm sure you'll tell me there's no truth in this?"

Pitt watched as Jones clenched and unclenched his fists. Here was a man always close to the edge, the kind of individual locals would be careful not to upset by spilling their pint on his suit or stare more than a split second at a girl he might be with. Jones did not answer as Pitt continued;

"Let me put it to you like this Mr Jones: In the course of your brotherly evenings out, maybe a game of pool or darts and a few pints of lager, did your brother ever mention the fact that all of the cottages in the row are interconnected via the roof space and that therefore it would be easy to access any of them by simply entering the empty building at the end of the terrace?"

Jones was clearly taken by surprise by the line of questioning but very quickly recovered his previous aggressive stance.

"Of course we talked about it, mainly because bloody King was makin' out he was doing everyone a big favour. Okay yes, he paid a fair slab but he'd convinced the daft old buggers in the block that the price was cheap. He ripped 'em off and got a back 'ander from the gaffer. Andy heard 'em talking about it. King made five hundred quid out of it and the old folk thought the sun shone out of his arse. Bloody stupid they are. It was nothing to him, just a bit of petty cash. He just did it because he was an evil bugger who liked to put one over on people. He wanted to buy up the rest of the cottages in any case and it would put him in their good books if they wanted to sell up and go into a home or something. Well he won't be doing that now will he?"

"No, he most certainly won't Mr Jones. Thank you for that frank analysis. Perhaps you could now explain why your fingerprints are all over the empty cottage and your footprints are also to be found in the property. Also, we have found your DNA on the mallet used to kill King."

This time, Jones was clearly rattled. His eyes reddened as he pushed at the table.

"I'm saying nothin' else until you get me a solicitor. I know my rights. You've no right to check my DNA. I haven't been asked for a sample anyway."

Pitt halted the interview and phoned the front desk.

"You'll have representation in half an hour Mr. Jones. Until then, relax and think about your answers. I'll have someone bring in tea and biscuits. "

Jones merely scowled as Pitt left the room. No DNA samples had been taken but Pitt had used the ploy many times. After the numerous stories in the papers of age-old crimes being solved using DNA, many perps were fearful at the mere mention of the technique. He was aware of its limitations but if the bad guys believed it to be a silver bullet, then so be it. Doctors are well known for using placebos which often give the required effect. To Pitt, this was a similar subterfuge. You use whatever ace you may have to put them where they belong.

Pitt knocked on the door to the adjoining interview room, entered and motioned to Khunkhun . In the corridor, they discussed how far each had progressed.

"Andy Jones is certainly not the full bunch of bananas Guv. It didn't take long for me to crack him. I used the DNA bit as we said. Scared him shitless, especially when I told him that we'd probably be charging him with conspiracy to murder. Within five minutes, he was spewing it all out. He claims that he and his brother had planned a robbery. They checked out the empty cottage together but he was the one who was going to get into the middle cottage because he knew the owners were away on holiday. They were both deliberately wearing identical clothes in case he was spotted and at the time they had agreed for the robbery, his brother would make himself known in the crowds at the festival and impersonate Andy. They are very much alike as we can see apart from the fact that Andy has a bit of a cut under his eye. It's almost healed now but it must have been quite deep so young Dean contrived to mingle wearing a large plaster under his eye. This went on for about half an hour or so during Dean's break. He'd been at the bar for about six or seven hours by then so it wasn't as if he wouldn't have taken a break. Anyway, young Andy squeezes through the gaps in each wall until he's above the middle cottage. He's just about to open the trap door when he hears this scream. He couldn't tell where it came from but in view of what we now know, he guesses it was from the brewery. It probably wouldn't have been heard down in The Green Man, the noise in the bar at that time was pretty loud. Up in the loft though he says it echoed. Says it was just like one of those supernatural slasher movies he watches with his brother. Nasty! He was scared to death and scrabbled back into the end cottage. End of story, no goods to fence, a waste of time and effort, and one shit scared would-be criminal mastermind."

"What do you think Jaz?"

"Funnily enough I do believe him and anyway he's just too thick to make up a tale like that."

The DCI scratched his head for a moment and then;

"I guess we'll let them go Jaz but let's soften them up in case we need more information. Just tell him some story about consulting the CPS before we decide to take it further. It's just not worth the effort and the paperwork to proceed with the attempted robbery and we've got more important work ahead. We'll just keep 'em wondering, eh?"

On his return to room 12a, Pitt found that Dean Jones had been joined by a man Pitt knew well and loathed with a vengeance. Gervase Smythe-Jenner LLB (Hons) was whispering confidentially in Jones's ear. He sat, hair slicked back, horn-rimmed spectacles. Inevitably he wore one of (as Pitt believed) his many black finely tailored suits. His expensive pair of leather shoes were shined to perfection. Obviously a major investor in Cherry Blossom black shoe polish thought Pitt.

"Before we start Pitt, let me tell you that I've heard this young man's story and I am of the opinion that in the furtherance of justice, I shall take on his case on a pro bono basis."

Hmm, I bet you will, Pitt thought. This was a murder case and the publicity engendered would be free advertising for law firm; Poulter, Smythe-Jenner. The man and his partner were vultures, ever ready to leap in should there be the possibility of headlines locally or nationally. They were well known ambulance chasers, a professional slur maybe but one which applied in his case. Pitt had spotted him on several occasions soliciting for clients at disaster sites, a vulture feeding off others' misfortunes.

"Very public-spirited Mr Smythe-Jenner. I'm sure few would be so generous. However, for the moment, we have no further questions for Mr Jones so possibly you may want to drive him back to The Green Man and save the taxpayers the cost of a police car?"

The solicitor angrily pushed back his chair, stood, and smoothed down his jacket before glaring at Pitt.

"Perhaps next time DCI, you will ensure that I'm not dragged away from an important case on a fool's errand,"

"I most certainly will but of course, we didn't ask you to be involved. I believe your client invited you."

As if performing on the stage at the local amateur dramatic society, Smythe-Jenner snatched his previously carefully arranged documentation from the table and stuffed the wad into his over large briefcase. He declined the hand proffered and marched out into the corridor allowing the swing door to close on his client.

"Very bad manners and that from a man of the law," Pitt murmured. It had made his day.

Chapter 20

The sky was overcast and a little rain was predicted for later; a very good day indeed for any funeral. The church service had been brief. The bearers, a group of Raggy Men, directed by Jim Walsh had carried the coffin to the altar not as Pitt had expected to the accompaniment of one of their favourite dance tunes but to a rendering of Paul McCartney singing 'The long and winding road.' An impressive cross of red roses with a sash that read: 'To my only love from your wife Bella' embellished the lid. Bella King maintained the charade that Pitt guessed she had perfected over many years. Few villagers were impressed and the occasional tutting sound could be heard as the flowers were inspected. What might to an outsider have seemed an outpouring of grief at the death of a loved one, to the villagers smacked of rank hypocrisy and they were not fooled for one moment.

The artistically personalised order of service card showed Tom King looking happy and handsome and just a little 'photo shopped' whilst standing on a rugged hillside surveying all below him. Listed were prayers, ministry of the word, a tribute by Jim Walsh, more bible reading (John Chapter 14), and so on. Pitt thought that the priest seemed too young for the job. He gave the impression that he might have come straight from a seminary after passing whatever exams were necessary for funerals, weddings and baptisms. He was therefore still overly fresh and eager to conduct his first funeral service though still a little nervous. Perhaps he wanted to show the small group of mourners that he was well versed in modern customs. Whether a sermon based on a 1970 Beatles hit could in the second decade of the new millennium be classed as 'trendy' Pitt could not be sure.

Nevertheless, the young cleric proceeded on his 'journey'. We can see he said that life is a long and winding road and there were he explained many turnings. Some led to a good and Christian life whilst others led to darkness and the inevitable decline into wickedness. He had it on good authority (looking directly at Mrs. King) that Tom King had been a paragon of virtue in this life and had now surely ended his journey with a place in Heaven. The young man seemed to have an inexhaustible supply of holy water with which to douse the coffin and then with a swish of his cassock, he led the procession out of the church and into the daylight. A CD. played.

"Layla, you've got me on my knees. Layla, I'm begging darling please."

Whether Eric Clapton was Bella's choice or a favourite of her late husband, Pitt had not the faintest idea but once more, he had certainly never heard it played in church.

Pitt and Khunkhun stood a little way back from the mourners. Both though clad in heavy woollen overcoats were beginning to feel the chill wind blowing across the graveyard. The break in the weather seemed to coincide with the nature of the event. Perhaps tomorrow, the sun would shine once more. They watched as the small group around the freshly dug grave went through the age-old ritual. The priest was also feeling the chill and was no longer as enthusiastic in carrying out the service as had previously been the case. In fact, Pitt was aware of the occasional ripple of his vestments as the man shuddered with cold. His words were mumbled and recited as if by rote at an ever-increasing speed. Had Pitt not been to so many similar interments as part of his work over the years, he would have neither heard nor understood the words. As it was, he was aware that he was reading the priest's mouth rather than trying to discern his speech.

"Forasmuch as it hath pleased Almighty God of his great mercy to take unto himself the soul of our dear brother here departed, we therefore commit his body to the ground; earth to earth, ashes to ashes, dust to dust; in sure and certain hope of the Resurrection to eternal life, through our Lord Jesus Christ; who shall change our vile body, that it may be like unto his glorious body, according to the mighty working, whereby he is able to subdue all things to himself."

There was a mumbled 'Amen' blown away on the breeze. Grouped around the coffin, Pitt counted perhaps eight or nine men with beards, all holding up their Morris sticks in salute. The group was completed with the addition of Dean Jones, Tracey the barmaid and swathed darkly from her black leather boots up to a black full brimmed hat with a heavy veil, 'the grieving widow', Bella King. You can bet the underwear's black as well thought Pitt. Bella using what seemed to be a piece of kitchen roll received a handful of earth from Dean to be sprinkled upon the coffin. The action was followed with a tenderly placed blood red rose. She stood perfectly still for a moment, tall and elegant, head bent slightly as a mark of respect, then turned away and producing a delicate looking embroidered handkerchief from her clutch bag dabbed her eyes. The wind snatched at her veil and before she had retrieved this, mourners caught a glimpse of her serene and beautiful face. It was all pure theatre and well-rehearsed thought Pitt. The floral cross had been moved to one side of the grave and would be placed on the mound of soil later once the gravediggers had completed their work.

From what Pitt had heard 'on good authority', many wished that King would in fact be burning in hell whilst being pinched and poked by a thousand demons. Those now ringing the coffin with their heads bowed behaved as though they had lost a loved one. They did what was expected but with little genuine feeling.

Then suddenly, it was over. It was all a bit like the build-up to Christmas and then the emptiness when the day actually happens. Pitt and Khunkhun watched as the mourners led by Bella King, gently supported by Dean Jones, made their way back to the lych gate. Jim Walsh stayed awhile, bending to read the inscription on the cross then joined them as they snaked their way along the path. They would walk the short distance to The Green Man where a wake would be held. The officers followed at a distance. Just as the widow had left the graveyard, Pitt noticed a rather tall, well-built man climbing out of a sports car. He was perhaps of middle age and slightly balding. The car had been parked in the driveway in a position that demanded attention from those attending the church. The black prancing horse logo immediately identified the car as a Ferrari in bright gleaming red.

Bella King was staring fixedly in the man's direction. She stopped and turned to the group indicating they should carry on without her. Dean was waving his hands in a manner that told Pitt that he thought he should stay with her. Eventually, all, including Dean, moved on to The Green Man. Pitt and Khunkhun did not follow but watched from a distance at what followed. The church doorway was a convenient place to view and the darkness meant that they would not be seen by the couple who were now in deep discussion.

The man suddenly faced them. His features were clearly visible to the officers whilst at the same time, the blackness surrounding them meant that he was unaware of their interest. The effect on Pitt was certainly not what Khuhkhun had expected

"What is it guv? You look as though you've had a bad curry."

Pitt whispered in reply.

"I never thought I'd see that bastard ever again Jaz but here he is in of all places Upper Egginton. Just watch and when they've gone, I'll explain."

The man was gesticulating and pointing a finger in the direction of The Green Man. The black overcoat with velvet collar raised against the chill looked expensive but was cheapened by a blaze of bright redlining. Bella retreated, clearly alarmed. Pitt put a hand on Khunkhun's shoulder aware that his subordinate was about to intervene.

"Let it go Jaz, he's not going to try anything in broad daylight and I'd like to see what it's all about."

She backed away from the stranger and head down, hurried towards the safety of the pub. The man unbuttoned his coat, pulled down his collar, and climbed into the sports car. Clearly, the machine was meant for a smaller man but Pitt knew that only a Ferrari would suffice for a man with the ego of Nial O' Shaughnessy. Then he was away with blue smoke issuing from twin exhausts and an ear-splitting booming roar like a jet aircraft. A shower of stone chippings was hurled from spinning rear wheels. As he passed Bella, he hooted, wound down the passenger side window and shouted something. Bella broke into a run and pushed open the pub door. It was as if she were seeking sanctuary. The sacred place however was no church or temple but an English country pub. A moment later, Dean Jones appeared, face blotched red with anger but by then O' Shaughnessy had left the village.

Pitt was stabbing numbers into his 'I Phone' and murmuring to himself. Khunkhun could hear the odd word or phrase: "Incredible!"; "Can't believe this." and then he was speaking quietly but firmly.

"Yes Nial O'Shaughnessy, Fred. I'm sure it's him. Just appeared in darkest Shropshire. What's the word on the street?"

Pitt listened and after an interval of ten or so minutes, rang off and pushed the phone back into his inside pocket.

"Jaz, that lady just doesn't understand the danger she's in."

Chapter 21

Jim Walsh was all agog. His excitement bubbled over and he broke into a few steps of his favourite Morris dance. His long-suffering but understanding wife insisted he sit down and finish the full English she had prepared for him. Under normal circumstances, the bacon, eggs and mushrooms followed by toast and his favourite Frank Cooper's thick-cut marmalade would by now have been wolfed down and he would have been slurping down his coffee. Today Jim Walsh seemed to have morphed into what any grown-up weaned on The Magic Roundabout would recognise as Zebedee, the Jack in a Box. It was one of those days which if Jim could control his emotions, he might steady his hand sufficiently to make an entry in his diary, possibly underlined and even using capitals.

Bridgnorth's Pageant organiser had phoned just a quarter of an hour ago and during the intervening period, before returning to his breakfast, he had contacted half of the Raggy Men. The rest either weren't answering their phone when Jim's name appeared on the screen or were out. Jim of course would never have thought that any of his merry band would ignore a call from the leader. In one case, there did seem to be a genuine problem with the landline and contact using the mobile phone did not result in any better outcome. Jim would have to make a personal appearance. In any case, Jim needed to find someone to share his excitement with, face to face.

Jim's wife had entered the room just as he was making his last call.

"Yes Dave, we've been asked to fill in at the Pageant. Half of the Bridgnorth Vikings have gone down with some kind of virus and are spending their lives currently in the loo. Serves 'em right! Whoever heard of Morris dancers being named 'Vikings'? Authenticity is what it's all about not dancing around in horned helmets twirling wooden axes. Yes, it may be commercial and yes, they get the invites but tell me; Is it art? Is it culture? Is it keeping the tradition alive? Anyway, we're on but we don't have much time to rehearse. I need to get in touch with everyone today. You'll be okay, yeah? Great then, it's next week. Maybe we'll meet on the castle ramparts but I'll firm up with you on that one. We're scheduled to be on at two forty-five. Byee!"

His wife beamed. Jim wanted her to beam and to make as though she was totally overcome by the honour of having Jim's Raggy Men dancing at this major carnival. She was genuinely happy for him and proud to share in his reflected glory. There would be plenty of press coverage which in turn would lead to more 'gigs' although her husband would have choked on his bacon at the use of the word.

"Sorry love can't stop, people to see, got to get things organised. Can't have anything go wrong on this one."

He snatched a piece of toast, licked the butter from his hand, and bit into the still-warm slice. His wife helped him on with his special blazer. Jim's wife had carefully sown his personally designed badge onto the breast pocket. Jim was proud of the embossed shield emblazoned with the crossed Morris sticks and curls of gold wire. Then he was out onto the drive and without checking for traffic, had reversed his somewhat unreliable car into the lane. Jim Walsh was normally the most careful of drivers and often annoyed his wife with his tendency to be over-cautious when at the wheel. Today traffic was not on his mind. He had four calls to make; urgent calls which would bring fame to the Raggy Men.

Chapter 22

The ditch had been taped off and a squad car parked to the side. Two uniformed policemen had been positioned to move on any inquisitive passers-by. Walkers seldom trod the lane and only rarely would other traffic need to pass that way. Very occasionally farm lorries, harvesters, or maybe one of the council's tree lopping and hedging machines might be seen. Though cars would normally be infrequent, once the news of the find was passed on, Pitt was aware that he would be joined by the usual assortment of gaping ghouls and local journalists. There were no farms or private houses as far as the eye could see along that stretch. Death had visited a lonely place.

He lifted the tape and peered down into the drainage ditch. On the one side to a foot or so below the banking, the slimy mud had been smoothed out and imprinted. Looking into the trench, Pitt could see a slurry of brackish brown water on which lay a torpid flotsam of leaves and grass. Nothing moved in the stagnant brew. The body lay face down in the mire and he could just make out in the gloom an ugly splintered gash at the back of the head. It was of irregular shape and reminded Pitt of opening a tin can with a particularly blunt can opener.

It was apparent that the corpse had been slid down the bank. Little care had been taken and no attempt made at concealment. This was rubbish to be disposed of not unlike an old bedstead or washing machine not worth repairing, dumped to avoid making the journey to the local waste disposal unit. A cyclist suitably enclosed in black Lycra and wearing a swept-back helmet had come upon this bizarre human litter early that morning. The man who had made the grim discovery was talking to the constables, gesticulating and periodically hanging his head and rubbing his face. Pitt guessed the man was explaining how he had come upon the victim. He could imagine the man approaching from the same side of the lane as the culvert, head thrust forward over his handlebars. The body would certainly have been visible to him and he had abandoned his bicycle perhaps a yard or so from where the remains lay. The cyclist had used his mobile phone to call the local police in Bridgnorth.

By now the preliminaries had been completed; head and hands carefully bagged and the Scene of Crime officers signalled that the cadaver could be removed. The mortuary van was parked just outside the taped off area to avoid destroying any tyre marks which might be found by the SOCOs. The body was being gently lifted from its slime-filled resting place for insertion into a zipped black body bag. Bracelets of weeds hung from the legs almost as though the murderer had wished to embellish his deed. The officers watched; arms folded. For the moment there was little they could do apart from reading the cyclist's account of his find. Pitt's memory tracked back to the many times he had been on hand to watch an act which would eventually lead to that last journey onto the dissection table. His reverie came to an abrupt end when Jaz suddenly started forward, signalling for the bearers to halt their work. Something had caught his eye.

"Just a minute!" he called.

The man's once pristine blazer and grey slacks oozed liquid mud and greenish algae and as the body was turned and dragged towards the bag, Jaz recognised the face now gazing sightlessly towards the heavens.

"I'm not sure guv but I think this is one of those Morris people who we were due to interview. I just happened to be passing when the uniforms were taking down details and he stood out as he was being a bit bolshie about having to wait in line."

"Get the lads to have the group ready for interview and check if one has gone AWOL. There has to be some connection between King's murder and this one and so far the only match if you're right is that both were what do you call 'em; Raggy Men?

Chapter 23

The body had been identified as that of Jim Walsh by his stunned, grief-stricken wife. On returning home accompanied by Pitt, Khunkhun and a woman police officer, she once more gave way to wave after wave of misery. Mrs. Walsh's reaction to the news of her husband's death was in keeping with what Pitt had experienced so many times. Later on, as she viewed her husband's body, the contrast with that of Bella King's bland unfeeling visit to the mortuary was stark indeed. The colour had drained from her features to be replaced by a ghostly pallor when her husband's face was revealed. There had been a look of total disbelief and the need to convince herself that there had been a mistake. Surely the appalling, ice cold thing before her was not really her husband but some stranger.

On entering what had been the safety of her own home, she had given a little gasp and reached out blindly for a nearby chair to steady herself. Pitt needed to ensure she was safely seated before he would discuss the circumstances and to that end he had taken the precaution of having WPC Freda Townley on hand to assist him. The DCI signalled to Townley and she gently guided Mrs Walsh towards a sofa, sat beside her and placed a comforting arm around her. Khunkhun took up a position towards the rear of the group. Pitt and Khunkhun allowed Townley's magic to take effect. She skillfully managed to avoid the immediate topic and after a few minutes of idle chatter about children, pets, and the home generally, Freda suggested she might bring Mrs Walsh a cup of tea. The latter nodded her assent and directed the WPC to the kitchen.

Pitt resumed control. His usual method would be to describe Walsh's death as suspicious. In his experience, the word 'murder' was one to be used after those left behind had become accustomed to the fact that all was not as it should have been with the death. Nevertheless, in this current situation, he needed information and he needed it urgently.

"Mrs Walsh. I have to ask questions that every policeman needs to ask in matters associated with unexplained death. Please search your memory and think of anyone who might wish to harm your husband. Under different circumstances, we might have treated this as a random attack. We have yet to locate his car and it could have been that he was the victim of a mugging and vehicle theft and we cannot discount that possibility. However, in view of the fact that it has been just a week or less since Mr King was murdered, it could well be that the crimes are in some way connected. Your husband's body was found a mere two miles from The Green Man."

Pitt was relieved to see Townley entering holding a steaming mug of tea. Mrs Walsh clutched this with both hands seeming to draw comfort from its warmth. Freda had brought in a box of tissues she had found in the kitchen and placed it gently on the arm of the sofa next to the grieving widow. The latter peered at Pitt over the brim of the mug as if using it as protection against any further unwelcome news. Pitt continued.

"Your husband we are told, created the dance group, organised events and was in charge of just about everything. It was you might say, 'his baby'. Both men were members of a tight little club as it were. Could there have been any enmity between your husband and other members; you know jealousy or dissent over the running of things? Has anyone had some dispute with both your husband and Tom King?"

"No! No never! They all liked and respected him. He tried to make it a friendly team. Yes some of them had common business interests even though most were retired but it didn't impinge on the fun they had. Jim would never allow any disagreement over business. The Raggy Men were everything to him and nothing was more important than that they all get on well. Oh, dear! Oh, dear! Jim always looked after our finances. I'm really hopeless with money. Jim paid all the bills and the like. Oh, dear! How will I cope? "

She began to rummage down the side of the sofa and brought out two coins which she proceeded to examine in great detail.

"Oh, dear! Old pound coins. I shall have to try and get them exchanged at the building society. Jim would have done that."

Practical considerations had now begun to add to the sorrow of personal loss. She began to cry. Freda snatched a tissue from the box and pressed it into her hand. Jessica Walsh was a short squat lady; her face plain and lacking any makeup bar for a smudge of lipstick. Her eyes were of an insipid blue and her greying hair was snatched back from her face. Each sob resulted in her pendulous breasts, currently imprisoned in a baggy Fair Isle sweater gently moving from side to side. Pitt felt sorry for the woman. Her husband must have been her guiding light and he sensed a kind of adoration for the man emanating from Mrs. Walsh. Yes, what indeed was she to do when the fulcrum around which her whole life revolved was now gone forever. She was not a physically attractive woman and Pitt guessed she never had been. Marriage to her popular and motivated husband must have seemed a major catch for her. As she spoke, the wattle below her chin moved up and down. Pitt was reminded of those days long ago when he was asked to make up a foursome. It had sometimes been the case that when one of his friends had suddenly found a new girlfriend, a second male was required for her best friend. After much cajoling and promises of free beer, he would with much trepidation, fulfil the role. He had often ended the evening with the 'plain Jane' whilst his friend walked hand in hand with some ravishing young female. Mrs Walsh must have been just such a plain Jane.

"I'd always wanted to run a little cafe you know; fancy cakes on nice plates, tea in real china cups and old-fashioned teapots. Nice fresh flowered tablecloths and napkins and chintz curtains around the windows. Jim had found a lovely one for me in Bridgnorth in the High Town; a bit run down but just ideal for me. He was going to sort out the finance; said he needed to talk to one of the group about it. Don't know why but Jim was like that, always dealt with business to avoid me worrying. With a bit of TLC, I could have made it a place where people would feel welcome."

There it was again thought Pitt; money. Is this all about money?

"Mrs Walsh, I have a favour to ask of you. We could go through channels but that would slow down our investigation. Could we please go through your husband's financial records?"

Indecisive by nature, Jessica began to clasp and unclasp her hands. Townley stepped into the breach. Pitt was later to reflect that the woman was an absolute gem. She said,

"I'm sure Mrs. Walsh will not object and whilst you're doing that, Jessica and I can make a few phone calls to the children. Best to get that over with as soon as possible and break the sad news I always think. Is that alright with you dear?"

Jessica Walsh needed someone to make decisions for her and though there was no reply, a slight nod of her head signified her assent. Pitt and Khunkhun were directed to a large grey metal filing cabinet. Mrs Walsh gently pushed away a bloated, menacing-looking grey cat perched lazily on the window sill. She rummaged around beneath an ornate flower pot containing a huge spider plant and seemed relieved that she was successful in finding a key. It was obvious that she had never needed to unlock the cabinet before; this was a male domain.

They had been working through the papers for perhaps an hour. Pitt lay back in the chair, yawned, and stretched his arms. This was the kind of thing he would leave to his subordinate. Jaz had the training and like a bloodhound could sniff out what to others would remain hidden in reams of paperwork and lines of figures.

"Take a look at this guv."

Khunkhun had been thumbing through a lever arch file crammed with bank statements. He had scrutinised entries as far back as three years. In the September of that year, Walsh had cashed in a tranche of Marks and Spenser shares and as a result, there was an entry of seventy-five thousand pounds; a substantial sum. The following week, an identical amount was paid out to a Mr. Jackman.

"What is even more interesting is the security for Jackman's loan. I sifted through some more of the bumf in the filing cabinet and found a promissory note for the seventy-five thousand pounds with interest at five per cent per annum. The note is now due for repayment."

"Ding dong Jas, he's one of the stick and bell shakers isn't he? Follow the money Jaz; follow the money."

Pitt had always been of the opinion that rather like sharks, once money had been introduced into humanity's sea, the feeding frenzy often knew no bounds.

Chapter 24

Peter and Claire Jackman lived in a modest Seventies semi-detached house on the outskirts of Bridgnorth. Khunkhun concluded it was one of those respectable developments post-war baby boom couples aspired to and that their parents could never have afforded to buy. The style was what might be described as neoclassical Sixties shoebox; stark, square, purely utilitarian and small. The outside had changed little apart from perhaps the inevitable more recent white double glazed, plastic-framed windows and matching UPVC door all of which looked remarkably fresh and clean. For all of its blandness, Khunkhun mused that if this house had a personality, it would have been smug and self-satisfied. Just look how I've come up in the world with my superior front door. The handkerchief-sized front garden contained a lawn mowed to within an inch of its life and borders filled with regiments of pansies. The lawn's centrepiece was an overflowing green tinged concrete bird bath from which a forlorn stone figure of a bird of unknown species stared out. Khunkhun suspected that might be the only kind of avian that had ever bathed in its confines. The Jackmans seemed preoccupied with birds. On either side of a small fish pond, protected by chicken wire, beady eyed metal herons stood on one leg surveying the garden. Khunkhun guessed that goldfish might lurk in the murky depths. A pea gravelled drive led to an up and over garage door. The garage was just about suitable for a small car, a Ford Kia maybe and Khunkhun could imagine there being room for a workbench with walls festooned with tools hanging from masonry nails all of course in perfect order.

The officer parked the car on the road. The entrance to the drive was guarded by an elaborate wrought-iron gate topped with arrowheads. To the side, a glossy white picket gate was available for pedestrian entrance. He opened this, stepped inside, and allowed the coiled spring to close it behind him. Khunkhun crunched his way along the drive before ringing the doorbell. He heard the click of a chain being removed. The slightly wrinkled face of a middle-aged lady, who Jaz assumed was Mrs. Jackman appeared in the doorway. The gap was just sufficient for her to decide whether it was safe to allow access. She seemed nervous.

"Yes?"

Khunkhun proffered his warrant card. She eyed it suspiciously as if the hand held something more menacing. Eventually, she took it. After first glancing at the photograph, then at the officer, she opened the door and indicated that he should enter. Inside was simple, clean and welcoming and Jaz could smell fresh washing, tile cleaner, and pine air freshener. He was ushered into a through kitchen-dinner and noticed the inevitable wood burner. Why does everyone have wood burners? He mused. Before taking a seat, he said;

"It's your husband I really need to talk to Mrs Jackman. Is he at work? If so, I can come back later."

She looked towards the French windows and waved her hand, a gesture that seemed to say 'all mine' and replied,

"He's at the end of the garden. You can't see him from here. We have one of the longest gardens in the street. We are so lucky in that respect. He's finished early today so he's out there doing a bit of weeding in the rose garden. We like to keep things nice. He's really worried about aphids on his roses you know. Still, he's bought some special spray from B & Q which should do the job"

"Yes, I believe they can be something of a pest,"

Khukhun replied thinking to himself; aphids are the least of this man's worries.

She signalled to an armchair covered in a colourful cloth giving the appearance of a flourishing flower garden. Khunkhun observed that the whole room, especially curtains and wallpaper was also pure one hundred percent floral Laura Ashley. He made himself comfortable in readiness for the arrival of Peter Jackman. There followed a rather embarrassing silence. He could not help thinking that in this habitat where flowers grew in the garden and on the furniture, even Mrs. Jackman was now beginning to resemble the drooping plant on Pitt's windowsill in the office.

A door to the rear of the house was suddenly flung open and there was an exaggerated sound of stamping feet. Peter Jackman was carefully avoiding bringing half of the rose garden into his pristine house.

"Lifted enough spuds for tonight and I've got a lovely cauli for us, Claire. Just taking my boots off and shaking my jacket. Won't be a minute. I'll put the veg in the bowl."

Claire Jackman turned towards the door in anticipation. Her husband entered, smuts of soil on his nose, grey hair ruffled and sporting horizontal lines along each side of his head. Obviously, Jackman was a cap wearer when gardening and by the looks of it thought Khunkhun, he had purchased one a few sizes too small.

It was only when the officer arose to introduce himself that Jackman became aware of his presence and his immediate reaction was one of surprise.

"This gentleman is Mr Khunkhun Peter; he's a policeman and has called in to see you about something."

The atmosphere changed. Both Jackman's wife and Khunkhun had spotted the look of fear in her husband's eyes. His appearance was that of a man holding an unpinned hand grenade.

"DS Khunkhun sir and I'm here to ask a few questions about the deaths of Tom King and Jim Walsh. Rest assured, it's nothing official you understand so I won't be taking notes."

Khunkhun's attempt to ease the tension failed. Both husband and wife spontaneously flopped down onto a floral settee and proceeded to hold each other's hands. The grip was not one of comfort but one of dread. Jackman in particular seemed to squirm even more than his wife. A cat slinking away from an over-aggressive canine Khunkhun thought.

"However, this may become personal Mr. Jackman, so do you want us to be alone or is it okay for your wife to listen in?"

A fleeting storm cloud darkened Claire Jackman's face.

"I'm staying!"

Khunkhun noted the flush of anger. Perhaps she was not as meek and mild as had been his first impression. Her ragged nails were now pressed into Peter Jackman's arm. Jackman did not demur.

"Perhaps we could talk about Tom King first then. I gather that he was not too well-liked in the Morris group and some of the ill feeling was due to a dispute over land sales? Correct me if I'm wrong but the information from Companies House. You know the kind of thing, Annual Returns, Memorandum and Articles of Association? These show Tom King as being the major shareholder in what did you call the company.............?"

He flicked open his document wallet and made a great play of locating an official-looking certificate whilst at the same time observing the reaction of the couple seated opposite.

"Ah yes, here it is: 'Raggy Investments Ltd.' Obviously, the name implies some kind of linkage with your Morris group and in fact, in addition to Tom King we have smaller shareholdings for his wife and other members of The Raggy Men......................yourself included."

Claire Jackman loosened her grip and turned to her husband. This time there was no mistaking the passion.

"What is he talking about Peter? You've always told me that we have to be careful with our spending and budget wisely. How are you named as a shareholder in an enterprise with the likes of Tom King? You know how despicable he was and how he treated his wife. Where did the money come from? How much have you put in?"

The questions were coming thick and fast. There was no time for Jackman to answer the last one before another dart was aimed in his direction.

"I think I can answer that one, Mrs Jackman. This is a perfectly legal set-up and from what I gather, might even be an extremely rewarding one for you and your husband. Mr Jackman it seems obtained the money by way of a loan from Mr Walsh who as you are aware has also been murdered. You can understand I'm sure Mr Jackman, that with two of the investors dead together with the link to your dance group, it's important for me to interview those concerned with both the company and the group. As it turns out, with the exception of Mrs King, the rest of the shareholders are also Morris men."

Jackman was about to answer but before he could speak, Mrs Jackman, gimlet-eyed and frosty demanded;

"And how much exactly has my husband gambled officer?"

It was almost as though this was a dialogue between Khunkhun and Claire Jackman. Peter Jackman was not invited to take part. Peter Jackman had become invisible.

"It seems that Mr. Walsh provided a sum of seventy -- five thousand pounds as a loan."

"Oh My God! How much? Seventy-five thousand?"

Without warning, Claire Jackman's fists began pummelling her husband's face. Jaz leapt from his seat and grabbed her wrists. She lay back, moving as far away from her husband as possible and began to weep. Pathos had replaced anger. Khunkhun remained standing. He was now in a position of power and intended to take things as far as possible.

"You see the problem is this Mr Jackman: Walsh was in the process of investing in a cake shop for his wife. We find that his savings are all tied up apart from the loan to yourself. According to a document signed some three years ago the debt is now due in full together with an amount of interest and I'm wondering how you intended to pay this sum?"

"He..... he would have given me more time."

"I think you might be mistaken there sir; from what I hear from Mrs Walsh, the purchase was imminent so it would seem that he would have wanted the debt honoured immediately and in full."

Claire Jackman was now glaring at the officer. It was obviously a case of shooting the messenger when he brings bad news.

"Anyway, let us move on to Tom King. I'm told that King was holding out for a much greater figure than would ever be agreed by the development company. He was of the opinion that as the land held was the only access to the area to be built on, the longer he refused a deal, the greater would be the price paid. I am also led to understand that the shareholders, including his wife, wanted to sell but that he had a majority and refused to listen to the other investors. So you see my predicament, Mr Jackman? We have investors who need King out of the way in order to cash in. Then in your case, there is the added problem of Mr. Walsh wanting his cash ASAP otherwise he'd lose the café to someone else and thereby upset his wife."

Peter Jackman was overcoming his immediate jolt and was, at last, finding answers.

"This was supposed to be unofficial DS Khunkhun. I deeply resent your implied accusations. As to the loan, as I've said, I'm sure Jim would have found another way and in any case, with King dead, Mrs. King will sell and I'll have the money to pay back the loan plus interest and pocket a handsome profit for myself."

He glanced across at his wife in the hope of perhaps a friendly smile. There was no change in Claire Jackman's countenance. She had wiped away the tears and turned her head away from her husband.

"As you say Mr Jackman, you will at some time make a tidy profit as a result of King's death so that merely adds to the serious situation you find yourself in. Yes, this is unofficial but the situation will change if we cannot get to the bottom of all this. As to the loan repayment, it's a case of timing now, isn't it? With Jim Walsh dead there is obviously some leeway now. I dare say Mrs Walsh's dreams of a cafe are not now on the horizon. Quite obviously she's in no fit state to proceed with her business venture and in any case, she'll be unravelling the mysteries of legal mumbo- jumbo regarding wills or probate maybe, contracts, etc. It could all take months. Difficult for her but extremely fortunate for you as the last thing she'll be thinking about is demanding the money. As it is now, I dare say the shareholders will strike a bargain and your share of the cash will be banked before it becomes necessary for you to repay Walsh's loan. That makes things rather convenient I'd say, wouldn't you? Anyway, let's leave the matter there and I guess at some stage we'll need to continue this officially in our cabin outside of The Green Man. Thank you for your assistance. I'll let myself out."

Jackman was not intending to leave matters as they stood. The man was furious. The murder accusations were bad enough but the possible wreckage of his marriage loomed large.

"What you don't seem to have thought out DS Khunkhun is that I'm not the only person with a grudge against both King and Walsh. Maybe you'd like to start with Jakey James, 'Round Jakey' from the garage. He bought into the company and has as you are aware a small shareholding paid for from when he was employed as a mechanic for a company in Bridgnorth. Then he had the bright idea of going it alone and starting his own business. King owned the land and buildings, and loaned him money to start the business, equipment tools, and so on. The deal was that unless regular repayments were made, King would be entitled to repossess. I happen to know that the garage has not taken off as well as was expected. Jakey tends to drink too many pints of King's beer and then there's no stopping him from relating the sorry tale and telling us what a bastard King is, err was. He's tried time and time again to get yet another loan off Jim Walsh but Jim's just brushed him off. Worse than that, Jim being Jim, he tended to let him know what a fool he's been. On the face of it Jakey's a gentle cuddly teddy bear but I've seen him in one of his strops and believe me, you wouldn't want to upset him. Perhaps you can see where this is going? Oh, and by the way, perhaps you could ask him what he was doing following Jim's car on the day he was murdered."

There was a malevolent glint in Jackman's eyes. a kind of I'll show that bloody copper that I'm no soft touch look.

"That's very interesting indeed Mr. Jackman and you can rest assured that we are following up every lead. You can also be sure that we shall be talking to you again regarding this matter."

Khunkhun let himself out. He had no intention of making things easy for Jackman and in his view, the man was still at the very top of his list of suspects. As to Claire Jackman and her marital relationship, he had no idea whether those hand grenades were about to blow and what was more, he did not much care.

Chapter 25

During the train journey to London, Khunkhun reported to Pitt, Jackman's assertion that Round Jakey had as much to gain from the murders as he himself. For the moment, however, a follow-up would have to be postponed. There was a far more urgent matter to be dealt with.

Khunkhun surveyed his surroundings. So this is London? It was his first visit. Well, you can keep it he thought. Nearly two hours on a crowded train from Wolverhampton to Euston and a taxi ride across the capital where he occasionally spotted some rather sad looking landmark which never measured up to what he had seen on his TV screen. Crowds, crowds and yet more crowds. Every kind of nationality, dress and size. Humanity moving in a ragged flow to who knows where?

"Oh look, The Houses of Parliament guv!"

"Far more villains in the place where we're going Jaz" Pitt observed with a wicked smile.

It took Pitt back to his younger days and his trips to Soho to interrogate some cockney villain. He would be waved into some half-lit office; the decor being loosely based on a description in a Mickey Spillane paper back. The guardians of this inner sanctum would be a couple of ex or wannabe boxers or some greasy haired kid fingering a chiv in his inside pocket in a bold attempt to give an essential appearance of menace. Heavies who would do their master's bidding for a bone or two were ten a penny in London. They sprung up everywhere like weeds after rainfall.

Every city has an area where you would be deep into the oozing slime of gambling, drugs and prostitution. Some cities had given up the fight and had like Amsterdam and Nevada legalised the latter. In other parts of the world such as the Czech Republic, a complete country had declared it to be legal. Pitt had walked down those seedy litter-strewn streets and had come out the other side with a somewhat different view of humanity and the world. Women with too much red lipstick, the immovable firmness of silicone breast implants, or perhaps the huge and melon shapes for those specialist punters; the air of hopelessness seen through the eyes of a walking corpse. There were the inevitable pimps of all colours and nationalities in cars which probably cost two or three years of Pitt's copper's pay. Bars and clubs touted for custom on the basis of either topless or totally nude girls. Once inside and having paid a king's ransom for a watered-down lager, it was up to the punter, the girl and her pimp to decide how the night would proceed. Many young girls would come to London seeking what they imagined would be a Hollywood movie existence only to end up in Soho and its insatiable demand for young fresh meat. The vitality of Soho had been the vitality of a tumour. Pitt had been excited yet at the same time revolted by Soho.

Pitt introduced his subordinate to perhaps the greasiest of greasy spoon cafes.

"The best all-day breakfast in London Jaz. Just ignore the decor."

Khunkhun could not ignore the décor. Pitt had been seconded to the Met a decade or two before because of his specialist knowledge of some West Indian Brummie Yardy gang boss. The man had extended his territory into certain parts of the 'Smoke' resulting in a wave of knifings and shootings. He had spent more than twelve months as part of the investigation before returning to the Midlands and during that time had become well versed in the criminal goings on in the East End. All the old-style mobsters; the likes of the Krays, Tam Mc Graw, Mad Frankie Fraser and many more were of course long gone only to be replaced by a new and often better-organised list. Criminality abhors a vacuum they say.

Russians, East Europeans and West Indians had controlled the area previously the domain of cockney hard men and the enforcement of their suzerainty was brutal in the extreme. The small-time crooks were made to deal only with the heads of the mobs who in turn protected them from rival factions. It was a feudalistic criminal system that often resulted in the death of villains and resulting reprisals. Pitt was of the opinion that if one turned the occasional blind eye, then that trundling rusty old machinery which is the legal system would not be required. In a twisted kind of way, justice would eventually take its natural course. The millionaire perp would no longer need to employ the expensive services of some bent lawyer to find some technicality in order to beat the rap. It would not get that far; the man would be dead. Even so, he knew of scores of men allowed back on the streets who were in fact as guilty as sin but against whom it was impossible to make a watertight case.

Pitt had witnessed the birth of a new crime family before heading back to the Midlands. A young villain of Irish extraction had created an extremely efficient organisation by gathering together the remnants of IRA cells, deemed defunct after the Good Friday Agreement and organising them with military precision. There had been a dissident or two who had opted to go it alone but Nial (The Nail) O'Shaughnessy had moved quickly to assert his ascendency. Not for nothing was he known locally as 'The Nail'. What O'Shaughnessy could do, armed with just a nail gun was legendary. It was likely that the number of times he or his praetorian guard had used the tool was probably overstated. Nevertheless, whispers on the grape vine that some minor crook had been found just about alive with arms and legs stapled to a garage door for a trivial breach or suffered death by crucifixion for a major challenge to the leader had created an image in the criminal fraternity which was now legendary. As with ancient Rome, O' Shaughnessy tolerated only one Caesar in his East End criminal empire.

The same difficulty that the forces of law and order had found in trying to crush the IRA in Northern Ireland, abounded within The Nail's regime. He maintained the same cell-like structure as previously. The numbers involved could not be assessed and each unit was encouraged to report to him directly and no contact could be made between the various parts of his criminal jigsaw.

Chapter 26

Pitt's call to the Met had confirmed that O'Shaughnessy still ruled the East End with an iron grip. He had minions to do his bidding and enforce his demands; therefore, his personal visit to Bella King did not bode well for the woman. Pitt was going to meet his old friend DCI Fred Givens. The meeting would be on an unofficial basis and to that end, Zero Casabulis' (a.k.a. Zorba's) Cafe was ideal. They passed by a boarded-up shop doorway and a blanket covered sleeping bag which Khunkhun assumed contained one of London's many homeless people and made for Zorba's. An unsuccessful attempt at street art had been made on the boarding. Maybe the spray can had leaked.

Pitt, normally a healthy eater without being too fussy, occasionally succumbed to the lure of a full English breakfast. Today he intended to indulge himself. Zorba's all day English breakfasts were something to behold. Khunkhun glanced about him. Yes, the smell of sizzling bacon certainly got his gastronomic juices flowing and he was pleasantly surprised to see that though the rest of the cafe looked as though it had not been refurbished since the 60s, the cooking area was ultramodern, all gleaming stainless steel. Tables were topped with chipped red and black melamine and Jaz mentally prepared himself to hear some Rolling Stones hit being played over the sound system. Chairs were of a similar era with round plywood backrests attached to nickel-plated tubular frames and legs. Much of the silver had long since disappeared revealing rusty mild steel. The floor covering had once been matching red and black linoleum which over the years had morphed into a patternless grey. Khunkhun noted that even the solitary woodlouse wending its way across the flooring looked tired and dejected. Grubby-looking curtains clung desperately to their rails and the single glazed windows ran with moisture. This then was Pitt's culinary Utopia he thought. Give me Uncle Dagle's Red Fort Restaurant any time of the week. A slewed mirror had been attached to the entrance wall at a crazy height. He glanced at his reflection in the glass's smudged mist and sighed. Ah well, better indulge the boss.

Pitt had come back from the serving area holding in one hand three pairs of knives and forks wrapped in fresh white paper serviettes and a selection of condiments in the other.

"Push round Jaz, unless he's been on a Weight Watchers course, Fred Givens will need a considerable seating area to accommodate his considerable arse."

The cafe door swung open crashing against the adjoining wall and causing yet another small piece of plaster to fall to the ground and break into dusty splinters. Khunkhun noted that in a year or two the brickwork would be revealed. Fred Givens was indeed something to behold. His twenty-plus stone was encased in a huge double-breasted black suit which once might have been matt but which was now shiny. He used his weary-looking shoes to give an almost footballer-like back heel to close the door. Fred was obviously taking no risks with his trousers. In addition to tightness in the area that once might have been his waist maintaining these, he had taken the precaution of wearing a leather belt more suitable for cowboy style line dancing. Faded red bracers once considered essential in any movie involving a Wall Street trader were used as a secondary line of defence. His garish kipper tie hung from a bull-like neck covering a greying white shirt. London fashion's progress had come to a grinding halt way back in the Seventies and Eighties as far as Fred was concerned. The face was ruddy and large, eyes a faded blue, hair nonexistent.

Givens was the textbook idea of an old school hard man copper. Though Pitt, both in policing style and image was the South Pole to Givens' North, it was obvious to Khunkhun that his superior had great respect for this mountain of a man who plied his trade in what might be described as the black heart of the city. He was also Jaz thought, by the looks of him, a man with retirement tugging at his ankles. The two old friends greeted each other warmly, Pitt being engulfed in a huge bear hug.

"It's ordered Fred and I assume it's still the usual three spoonfuls in the coffee? I've brought my friend Jaz with me. He's 'sound' so whatever passes between us stays within the three of us."

Jaz and Fred exchanged the customary handshakes and the latter proceeded to squeeze himself into the gap between chair and table, sitting uncomfortably on a chair more suitable for the rump of a normally endowed individual.

"Ben, I could eat a horse!"

"Not on the menu I'm afraid Fred but I've ordered the next best thing for you mate."

The breakfasts and coffee arrived. Givens requested an extra piece of fried bread to add to the already overflowing plate. Jaz had to agree with his boss. This was a feast worthy of a trencherman.

Once the meal was in place, Fred Givens, mouth full of bacon and tomato, egg yolk dripping from one side of his mouth, leaned forward in a confidential manner. Jaz was aware that below those rheumy eyes was a globe of a nose which he might himself have fashioned as a boy using plasticine. This in turn was surrounded by a network of spidery red veins. Fred chewed as he spoke, now and then wiping the yellow yoke from his chin. He took a gulp of scalding hot coffee, grimaced and commenced.

"Nial O'Shaughnessy is a right hard bastard and don't give a rubber duck about us coppers. You were aware of him in his early days Ben but as the saying goes, like good wine, he's matured with age. In his case, maturity means fear and a style of evil quite unknown even to me. He's a bloody 'ard case alright. I guess even his own nightmares would be terrified of 'im. There's plenty around here who might suffer a heart attack just at the mention of his name. We should then ask ourselves how this murderous fucker got to end up in some secluded little village in Shropshire. Thatched roofs and babbling brooks are not his style and he's never given any suggestion that he'd like to be a local squire with a penchant for the odd stirrup cup and riding out to hounds. "

He took another slug of coffee and loaded his fork with a slice of sausage, mushroom, and a dab of tomato sauce.

"Years after you'd gone back Ben, his then trusted right-hand man decided the time was right to take a wedge of his leader's cash but also (and here's where it gets interesting) anything of value that was portable, then head for the hills and disappear. In normal circumstances, he'd have found the lad, maybe chopped off his fingers before torturing him for a day or two but this was completely different. This all happened whilst friend Nial was sunning himself plastered in factor twenty in his multimillion-dollar house in Majorca, surrounded by half a dozen beautiful girls ready willing and able to respond to his every need. So what does he do? He'd got a month's loot from his various business ventures (we guess maybe half a million) and leaves it with his ageing mammy who is confined to a wheelchair. His mother is the one weak spot in Nial's tough bastard make up. Can't do enough for her; always been a mammy's boy. Maybe a psychiatrist would have a field day asking him questions on that should he ever feel the need for therapy. Maybe we'd end up with one very dead psychiatrist in the event but it's worth exploring."

He roared at his own joke. Pitt grinned. Givens wiped a piece of bread around his plate, swallowed it, settled back a little, belched and carried on.

"So O'Shaughnessy's double-crossing Numero Uno spends time with dear old mum; looks to her every need and as she's in her late seventies and pretty doddery, there's plenty for him to do. In the meantime, he's locating Nial's stash and worse still, the family jewels. Nial's old man, long since passed on and now commemorated by a tombstone and a ten feet high concrete flying angel had been lavish in buying only the most expensive jewellery for his wife. Who knows how much it might be worth? Rumour has it a million wouldn't cover the bill. So whilst Nial's out there in Spain, directing his ladies to massage muscles aching from punching seven shades out of competitors, his man is quietly extracting money and sparklers from his mum's house. She's unaware of this and in any case, the old girl is not quite the full quid. She gets a message that he's ill and can't come over for a day or two whilst in actual fact, he's 'opped it with his swag bag to places unknown. Well, you can imagine The Nail's discombobulation when he finds out what's happened. We could almost hear his bellowing down at The Yard. We know that in this case, instead of delegation, he swears on The Mother of God that he'll cut the man's balls off. It gets worse in that the shock of what has happened gives his dear old mum a heart attack. Dead before she hit the floor!

Anyway, over the years, he's been using all of his contacts to find the man but without success. Your phone call got me thinking and when you started talking about the recently widowed lady, I put two and two together and hopefully made four. You said that the lady's name is Bella King and that her recently deceased husband was a Tom King? You could find nothing about his history prior to his arrival amongst the cow pats? Think on this; the geezer who took Nial O'Shaughnessy for a million-plus was Terence Kindle. Get it? T. K.; Tom King, Terence Kindle. You might think it's pretty stupid to take a name with such an obvious connection but it happens quite often. Whether it's an ego thing or to make remembering your new name easier, I really don't know. You say King was murdered in bizarre circumstances but even so, it's not O'Shaughnessy's style. However, it could be that one of his villains jumped the gun before Nial got on the scene. When he's not sunning himself with the bikini girls in Spain, he's doing the same thing but in Australia. Pity he hasn't been chewed up and spat out by a great white. Anyway, perhaps someone wanted to ingratiate himself with the Great Leader. If that is the case, they would be sorely mistaken. O'Shaughnessy wants to butcher Kindle and crisp him up on his hog roast. Take a look at these pictures Ben. They are well over ten years old but pretty clear."

Pitt examined the photos, and passed them on to Khunkhun who nodded in his direction. Tom King in a previous incarnation was Terence Kindle.

"It all makes sense Fred. One of O'Shaughnessy's mob does for King. O'Shaughnessy can't take it out on King but he does have the man's missus to go for, especially as he's worked out that some of his cash has been spent on the pub but that the bulk of it and maybe the family jewels must still be hidden away somewhere. I've got a very nasty feeling that unless his little tête-à-tête with the lovely Bella does not result in her producing sufficient goods and cash to satisfy him, she is in for a very unpleasant time indeed. Any chance you can stall him a bit, Fred? Sure to be something you can have him in for and give Jaz and myself time to sort things out at our end."

"I'll try Ben but these days, with him being virtually a tax exile, there's very little that we can pin on him. As to your pub gaffer lady, I think you need to take any threat to her very seriously indeed. O' Shaughnessy has dreamt up a very unpleasant end for his local toms who decide to leave his 'employment' or maybe spill their guts out to the Met. Whilst any self-respecting pimp would use the plastic bag over the head, Nial has his own unique method. He's figured out that most ladies carry a tampon in their handbag. He takes one, dunks it in water, rams it down their throat, and duck tapes the mouth. If he's really upset, that's the end of the matter. If on the other hand, he's in a forgiving mood, he grabs the cotton end and pulls the tampon out. Either way, no one's going to point the finger. We know it's him but what can you do? No proof."

Pitt eased himself up, Khunkhun did likewise.

"Gotta go Fred! Love to stay longer but after what you've just told us, we need to get back pronto, and thanks for the help."

Givens smiled, extended a greasy hand to both men and settled back signalling for another cup of coffee.

The return to Wolverhampton was immediately followed by a car journey back to Upper Egginton. Pitt needed to warn Bella King of the danger she was in. Okay, Terrence Kindle, Tom King or any of his many aliases was dead but somewhere there were considerable assets in both money and jewellery belonging to one of the most feared gangsters in London. Perhaps not being able to insert an injection of nails into King only exacerbated his ire and someone had to satiate his anger. Pitt indicated to Khunkhun that he leaves Mrs King to him whilst Jaz undertook a meeting with Round Jakey.

Chapter 27

Khunkhun could smell Jakey's place even before he had parked the car. He had driven most of the way with his windows half-open. It was just his luck to find that the only available car in the carpool had a dodgy air conditioning unit. On opening the door, he had been hit by a solid wall of heat and it took perhaps twenty minutes of parking in the shade and leaving all doors wide open before he could commence the journey. His annoyance was heightened further when he became aware that the windscreen wipers were in urgent need of new blades. Any attempt to clear away the debris of insect splatter as he sped on resulted in red arcs across the glass and a lack of visibility.

Until he had left the city behind him, the petrol and diesel fumes coupled with the heat of the sun produced a choking broth. Suddenly on approaching the countryside, the chemicals were replaced by the more acceptable odour of plant decay and horse manure. Khunkhun drove on with one hand on the steering wheel, the other searching for the bottled water he had brought with him. He unscrewed and took a hearty gulp, coughed a little, and felt refreshed. The heat steaming road lay ahead and then, there it was, the sign which read 'Jakey's Garage.' A smaller sign claimed that 'Jakey' provided both the 'cheapest and best Service and MOT in Shropshire.'

In the distance, he could see the broad bulk of a council refuse lorry and small figures darting to and fro loading up and then removing wheelie bins from the rear. The lorry ground on its way through the village and Khunkhun speculated as to how something that size could make its way along the narrow lanes to arrive at its current destination.

The garage was sizeable, just a little off the road and giving sufficient room to park perhaps three or four cars. The garage doors were fully open but nevertheless, there was a semi-darkness within relieved by the glare of a portable lamp dangling beneath what Khunkhun recognised was a Mini. He could make out a pair of feet extending from beneath the raised car and called out.

"Mr. James, I'm here on a police matter. Can you please come out for a moment?"

There was a loud grunt from beneath the vehicle and the sound of a gush of air released in a frustrated sigh from Jakey to be followed by a string of obscenities.

"Can't yer see I'm workin?"

Jakey pushed himself out, the wheels on his flatbed trolley creaking under his weight. He raised himself, pointed at the engine block suspended above the Mini and shook his head. Khunkhun was immediately hit by a waft of industrial strength aftershave which he could not immediately identify. Jakey's arms and a section of his face were highlighted in blue with tattoos of various designs. Having seen similar art on one of the Jones twins it was apparent that the local tattoo artist did a roaring trade.

"He's coming back fer that tomorrow. What yer want?"

The engine seemed to Khunkhun to be hanging precariously on a chain far too fragile for the weight involved. He produced his warrant card and introduced himself.

"It's probably best we discuss this in your office."

The officer nodded towards what looked like an enlarged broom cupboard with a single grease smudged window for light. The 'office' had been haphazardly constructed in the far corner out of random sized pieces of timber and a cast-off UPVC front door and frame. The outward appearance of this construction left Khunkhun in some doubt as to whether it would accommodate both himself and the mechanic's obese frame. Oily overalls hung by a single strap over Jakey's right shoulder and were stretched to breaking point over the area of his paunch; clearly, he had spent a few pounds on beer to achieve his fleshy frame. The material on his rear end had been patched and repatched with varying shapes and colours of material. Jakey grabbed a filthy rag, wiped the sweat from his brow and blew his nose loudly.

"Dust gets right up yer nose. I used ter take snuff ter clear it but I gave that up years ago."

In a manner reminiscent of a bull elephant charging an interloper, the man marched towards the office, his safety boots clattering on the concreted floor. In fact, the office was surprisingly spacious and Jaz had no difficulty in sitting on a threadbare armchair. Jakey had tossed a bath towel to him saying'

"Put that down first. Wouldn't want you ter get yer suit dirty."

Jakey sat behind what passed for a desk. Cut down railway sleepers were used for legs. These had been screwed to a length of plywood. He pushed aside a pile of papers and unopened letters muttering,

"Bloody final notices. They can F. off! Wana cuppa?"

Khunkhun declined as politely as he could having previously observed that the coffee mugs lined up at the side of the desk were stained a deep brown and judging by the spider webs of cracks visible were so close to death that he feared he may be left holding the handle as the cup disintegrated. Jakey boiled an electric kettle, taking care to avoid handling the bare wires sprouting from the lead. Before adding boiling water, he heaped a huge spoonful of coffee into his cup from a jar which proudly proclaimed itself to be 'My Instant Coffee.' Jakey looked at the officer and informed him,

"I like it black and strong. Now what's goin on?"

"Well it's like this Mr. James; we are investigating two murders in the village. You will be aware of this of course and also that both men were members of your dance group. We are interviewing all concerned but, in your case, it seems you had a special connection with Mr Walsh, not only with regard to your social life but also in respect of financial matters."

Round Jakey was beginning to take notice. His ears pricked up like a retriever scenting a game bird.

"I've certainly got a connection with Whitsun Willy, him and King loaned me the cash for this dump. Worst thing I ever did but it seemed a good idea at the time."

"We think it goes deeper than that though Mr James. Am I correct in thinking Mr Walsh needed the money to be repaid in order to finance his wife's new venture?"

"Yes, he was talkin about it but he never put any pressure on."

Khunkhun waited a while before his next question.

"Now the other problem that has come up Mr James is that you were seen following Mr Walsh's car on the day he died. Can you give me any reason why you might do that?"

James was furious, and on raising himself up from his chair, he inadvertently knocked over his mug of coffee. Khunkhun sprang back but nevertheless could not avoid the wash of hot coffee seeping through trousers and onto flesh. Round Jakey did not apologise.

"It's bloody Jackman isn't it? Yes, I followed 'im; 'ad to. His car was a piece of shit on four wheels. I kept it going for 'im long after it was clapped out. On the day he came around to tell me about Bridgnorth, he said he was goin around everybody, even them as he'd phoned. He was so bloody excited. I said to 'im; "Jim let me 'ave a look at the car. Wouldn't want you stuck in the middle a nowhere." So I spent about half an hour givin it the once over. I told 'im 'e'd got about six months before he'd have ter take it down the scrap yard. Then he left and I thought; best follow 'im just in case. So I did for about two or three miles. I seen Jackman at the crossroads and 'e seen me. He flashed me as I passed him. 'E was indicating to turn right which meant he'd be goin the same way. I turned off a mile later and never saw him again."

"No one who can verify that you didn't continue to follow him is there Mr. James?"

"No there aint apart from that bastard Jackman and he aint goin ter back me up now is he. He's always 'ated me. Reckons I'm lowlife, beneath him and all that."

Chapter 28

'Friday Night is Disco Nite at The Green Man. Do your thing to Fred Funk; good old-fashioned Soul, Motown, and a bit of Northern Soul. 7.30 pm till Midnight admission £3.'

King's death had not had any effect on the pub's entertainment. Friday night had always been disco night and so it would continue. As Bella King put it:

"It's what Tom would have wanted."

This would be taken with a whole shaker full of salt by those listening to the conversation. A pinch would certainly not have been adequate. Cars were lined up along the periphery of the village green. The night was warm, the doors and windows were ajar and villagers of Upper Egginton would be treated to lashings of Wilson Pickett and Mustang Sally, Four Tops, Sam and Dave et al. Those villagers who were old and frail or had been brought up on a musical diet of Doris Day closed their windows and curtains and mumbled about the 'noise'.

Pitt's arrival was heralded by James Brown performing 'Sex Machine' at a volume that Pitt mused might have made the pub's ancient timbers go into neurogenic shock. He parked in the first available space and made his way to the entrance. The temporary police station was in darkness but the light from the pub's doors and windows illuminated the village giving the age-old cottages a ghostly veneer. The building seemed to be breathing out great gouts of heat, catching the unsuspecting passerby with hot beery wafts. It took Pitt back to his own disco days. James Brown, eh? The Godfather of Soul himself.

He carefully avoided a man way past middle age, bellbottom trousers, shirt open to the waist revealing a gold-plated medallion, reliving Northern soul nights of long ago and still having the ability to spin on the spot as he headed for the bar.

Pitt caught the pungent odour of a spliff of cannabis being smoked somewhere in the throng. He was not visiting The Green Man to investigate some minor infringement of the law. Dodging in and out of the swirling mass of arms, legs and the many-hued faces constantly illuminated from the effect of bizarre speckled strobe lighting, Pitt spotted Tracey. The woman's slightly flattened face and large bulging eyes gave the impression of a cuddly lovable Pug. From the banter aimed in her direction, It seemed, as with Pugs that everyone cherished Tracey. She was in the process of angling a pint glass and heaving on a pull whilst at the same time making shouted conversation with a beer gutted man with straggly shoulder length grey sparse hair; obviously a regular. Pitt caught a snatch of the conversation. The man was evidently enjoying his evening.

"Luv Northern Soul Trace! Luv it!"

And then pointing to his frothy topped pint of Mild ale

"Err top it up luv. Short measure!"

Tracey held the glass to the bar's lighting, agreed and complied. The man paid, slurped a mouthful of beer, and disappeared into the writhing crowd of party people.

Pitt moved in before the man next to him who had caught her attention by waving a ten-pound note. He was young, muscular, and multi tattooed.

Tracey calmed the possibility of an altercation.

"It's okay Jono, it's a police matter."

Pitt glanced along the bar. In spite of the crowd waiting to be served, Bella King was nowhere to be seen.

"I need to speak to the boss on an urgent matter Tracey. Where is she?"

She gave a backward glance and pointed to the stairs.

"A bloke's turned up sounds like one of them cockney's off East Enders and she says she has to deal with a business matter. Picked a bloody fine night to leave the bar!"

She did not need to describe the visitor. There could be little doubt as to who Bella was entertaining in her office. Pitt was shocked; surely even O'Shaughnessy would not show his face when so many were in the pub? The man's swaggering self-esteem had always been apparent but even so...... Then of course this was the country not London and any gangster from the capital would believe he had little to fear from the local 'woodentops'. Pitt said no more and in a single movement, unlatched the bar gate, pushed it open, and ran for the stairs. Clearing the first two steps in a bound, his upward dash was halted by a chilling scream, followed by a grunt and a falling bulk that appeared to cartwheel down the steep flight. A body, curled into a huge ball-like shape careered into the officer hurling him backwards so that his head hit the wooden door frame. Pitt lay, stunned beneath a jerking twitching figure.

Then shaking away his shock, he raised himself gingerly from beneath the man. O'Shaughnessy lay, blood seeping from a wound in his chest. On closer inspection, the weapon used was still firmly embedded. From the look of the handle, Pitt guessed this was a letter opener, with a point which if used at close range could be a formidable weapon. He bent over the man and felt for a pulse in his neck. He could find none. O'Shaughnessy's sightless eyes stared up at him almost accusingly. There was nothing that could be done now for one of the capital's most feared villains and in Pitt's mind he was glad to see at least this one had got what he deserved. His job now was to speak to Bella King. He put in a call to Wolverhampton on his mobile phone, arranging for O'Shaughnessy's body to be examined on site then carefully brushed past the cadaver and climbed the stairs leading to Mrs. King's office. Jones was on his knees, one arm around a sobbing Bella King, whispering words of comfort to the woman who was clearly distraught. The usually totally controlled Bella was reduced to a shaking rather childlike figure. Pitt was first to speak.

"Please step away Mr Jones."

Dean Jones stepped back and Mrs King looked in the officer's direction. Gone now was the broken woman of a few seconds ago. She sat upright in her chair, dabbing at the smudged rivers of mascara staining her cheeks. Then suddenly she raised her right hand and pointed in the direction of Jones. Her voice was firm. The tone was almost that of some bewigged judge handing out justice.

"He did it! He stabbed him. I was trying to reason with the man but Dean lost control, lost his temper and killed him."

Jones moved towards her but Pitt manoeuvred himself between them.

"No! No! You know it wasn't like that Bella. Tell him. He was going to kill you if he didn't get what he wanted. You screamed for me to help. You know you did. Why are you saying these things?"

She turned away looking at Pitt rather than the younger man. Pitt nodded.

"I'd like you to come with me Mr Jones. Both you and Mrs. King will be needed to make statements and I'm afraid this will mean that you will be taken to Wolverhampton and I recommend that you both have a solicitor present."

In the lounge the music played on, the lights flickering on sweating dancers. In the bar, locals stared at catch-up TV, and Jeremy Kyle challenging a fat shaven-headed, bearded young man to submit to a lie detector test. It was it seemed necessary to prove that he was not the father of the sobbing waif-like girl Jeremy was clutching to his chest. Life went on in The Green Man whilst up above a man had been stabbed to death.

Chapter 29

Andy Jones was adamant. The duty sergeant tried in vain to avoid his gaze, shuffled papers in search of a non-existent missing document, and fingered his keyboard keys in mock computer work mode all to no avail. The man stood, immovable, both hands on the window sill. Here was an unbending object which no amount of suggestion or angry insistence that he should take a seat had the slightest affect.

"I want to see Pitt and I want to see him right now!"

The sergeant was accustomed to the awkward; the "I've had ten pints of eight percent rough cider; I'm pissed and am about to spew up over the floor" or the screaming woman, often resorting to spitting in his face but this one was distinctly icy. He could not be seen to give in and in any case, DCI Pitt was in the middle of interrogating the man's brother.

"It's important and has a major bearing on that bloke's death."

Andy Jones could not be talked into explaining. Andy Jones was intent on a communication with the organ grinder and the monkey could go f. off and play with his nuts. The officer sighed, relented, and pushing aside his computer keyboard, signalled to a passing constable. The man was immediately despatched to the interview room with a directive that he knocks quietly, wait for an answer, and inform DCI Pitt that Dean Jones's brother was claiming he had information relating to the suspect. Sometime later, Pitt, face a shade of molten steel, eyes blazing and using both hands, angrily slammed open the double doors allowing them to swing back unchecked. He ignored Jones and turned to the officer.

"What's going on here Jack? I'm right in the middle of a murder investigation."

Jack, looking sheepish, pointed towards the man now giving the impression of somehow being welded to his office window.

"It's his brother. Claims he's got information on the murder; tried to bugger 'im off but he won't go."

Pitt grimaced and gave a submissive nod in the sergeant's direction.

"Okay Jack, wheel him over to the corner table. I'll see if there's any mileage in what he's got to say before I take him down below. If he's full of crap, I'll boot him out."

He crooked a finger and directed Jones to a circular coffee table in the corner of the room well away from the hearing of other officers. He sat down and waited for the man to join him. He laid his arms on the table avoiding the grease spots left by the previous user. On finding it rocking and unbalanced, he reached in his pocket, produced a pound coin and slipped it beneath the offending table leg. The pair sat, each awaiting comment from the other. Pitt's already paper-thin patience was stretched to the limit. He took the lead.

"Right sir, as you are aware, I am a very busy man and I am as you are also obviously aware, in the process of taking a statement from your brother after which, in all likelihood, I shall charge him at the very least with manslaughter but in all probability with murder. So, let's cut the bull and you tell me what is so important."

Andy Jones did not like coppers and he particularly disliked coppers who he perceived were talking down to him. He fumbled in an inside pocket and retrieved his cigarettes, glanced at the gruesome picture on the packet and was about to open the flap when Pitt shook his head and pointed to a notice on the wall forbidding smoking. Jones pushed the packet back into his pocket and brought out a smaller one.

"Chewing gum forbidden, is it?"

Pitt did not respond and Jones fiddled with a packet of spearmint before loading a strip into his mouth and

132

chewing exaggeratedly. His anger resulted in a loud tirade expressed in heavily accented local dialect.

"I'll tell you what's important mate. Instead of trying to put my brother away, don't yer think yer might have a word with that bitch? She set 'im up, planned the whole thing; led 'im on. For months now, even before King got what was coming to 'im, she's been egging 'im on. "I'm getting a divorce Dean"; "I love you Dean"; "We can be together Dean." I told 'im, I said, it's a load of bollocks Dean but he wouldn't 'ave it. Like a little puppy round 'er feet he was."

Jones paused, took a breath, chewed on his gum, and continued,

"She told 'im that the bastard from London was some kind of contract killer, like on the telly. He believed 'er of course. The sun shone out of 'er arse and you just couldn't say a word against her. Bloody crazy! She told Dean that he'd threatened 'er after the funeral. Something about money, diamond rings and stuff that King had taken from his old ma. I don't know the exact details but it was something about, if she didn't make good his loss he'd do for 'er. She said that the bloke had found King after his picture was in a mag. King won some kinda CAMRA beer competition and his picture was in that CAMRA magazine. 'What's Brewing?' Reckoned King knew nothing about the photo 'cause they'd phoned 'er for one. Certainly buggered 'im up it did. The whole of the country would 'ave seen it. Ended up dead didn't 'e. Mmmm wouldn't surprise me if she knew about his past and dun it on purpose. She knew 'e was comin today; told Dean about it and said she needed 'im in case there was trouble. Oh course Dean jumped at it didn't 'e, bloody fool! It was just the same with King. She kept my brother on a string, told 'im all about it when 'e went into one of 'is blue fits; and no before you say it, my brother didn't kill Tom King. He'd certainly have wanted to many times and she put 'im in a position where it might have 'appened. She's a wicked old bitch that one and Dean fell for it every time."

Pitt eyed the man. He had listened but was not entirely convinced. Why wouldn't he want to protect his brother and yet what he was suggesting was certainly possible. On the other hand Pitt had seen the adoration on the young man's face. Bella King benefited from her husband's death and maybe she had also contrived to have Jones disposed of as a danger to her well laid out future plans. There could have been little doubt that she had expected trouble when O' Shaughnessy arrived.

"You can be sure that I shall be questioning Mrs. King on this matter as part of my investigation. As things stand at the moment, your brother has killed a man and I must now continue with questioning him. I will certainly keep you informed."

Jones declined the handshake, turned and headed for the door. He reached for his gum, spat it into his hand and pressed it onto the table top nearest to the exit.

Chapter 30

Dean Jones was held in Cell 2. Facilities were Spartan. There was a lavatory in the corner, wash hand basin, and a single bed but it was clean and did not have the smell of urine, vomit, and body odour that permeated the walls of the other dozen or so cells in Wolverhampton Police Station. Pitt had specifically instructed that he should spend his time whilst in custody in more salubrious conditions than was the case with many of the drunks, dossers and Saturday night brawlers whose normal overnight habitat was the police cells. In the meantime, a separate police car had brought Bella King in for questioning.

She was escorted through the doors by a young and obviously impressed police constable. Jack glanced in his direction, winked, and instructed that she come to the window and be entered in his book. With name, address, time and officer involved dutifully recorded, Mrs King was taken to a room that Pitt had used earlier in his interrogation of Dean Jones.

Khunkhun sat in on the interview. Mrs. King was informed of her rights once more. Bella King was certainly photogenic and had made a surprisingly rapid recovery from her trauma. In the time she had been allowed prior to the arrival of the panda car, she had changed into a stylish simple black dress cut to enhance the look of her shapely body and had ensured her makeup was fresh, not excessive, and suitable for what she might regard as a kind of business meeting. As ever, she was wearing her by now Pitt thought, trademark red shoes. He noted the outfit and the body language. Here was a lady who knew just about every trick in the female book. Here was a lady who would have not the slightest difficulty ensnaring some young impressionable country boy. Her perfume might have cost the equivalent of a week of his salary. Khunkhun and Pitt exchanged glances, the former's meaningful look was plainly designed to warn his boss but Pitt needed no such advice on this occasion.

"Are we saying that you have declined legal advice, Mrs. King?"

"Mmmm you've probably noticed that I'm a big girl now inspector and I really don't need some little chap pointing out the bleadin obvious to me."

Pitt composed himself and then began.

"Right then Mrs. King, if you are quite satisfied, I need to fill in a few missing pieces in this episode."

He continued at pace in the expectation of avoiding Bella King's expected exhortation to 'Call me Bella please Inspector.'

"What I need to understand is how Jones happened to be in the office at precisely the time that some London gangster came to see you. How is it that your barman was not serving behind the bar and was it seems sitting with you?"

King smiled one of her well practised radiant smiles, a little sunshine permeating the drabness of the interview room.

"Oh, that's easily explained, Mr Pitt. Now that Tom has passed away...................."

She paused, gave a peremptory sigh, brushed away an invisible tear, and continued,

"I need someone with a little knowledge of brewing and Dean was often left to take care of that side of the business by my husband. He's quite intelligent you know."

Not intelligent enough to see through you though thought Pitt.

"He was in my office for our weekly meeting with regard to how this week's brew was progressing. Obviously, it's a little too technical for me so I'm relying on him completely and just hoping that all will be well.

Wouldn't want to lose our reputation by giving our customers anything less than the best pint would we?"

Bella King was in full helpless female mode. Pitt tapped his biro on the table.

"I see, so Dean happened to be in your office for his weekly meeting with regard to the beer production at exactly the time that Nial O'Shaughnessy makes his way up from London and bursts into the brewery?"

Mrs King was wrapping a lock of hair around a finger, straightening it and pushing it behind an ear. The many facets of her diamond earrings sparkled in the light of the single bulb. She paused, seemed to think deeply, and replied;

"It does seem a very odd coincidence Inspector but I can assure you that I had no idea that this man was going to attack me."

Pitt flicked through the sheets of notes before him, stopping at one and pulling it closer to his face.

"You had no idea of what your husband was involved in when you met him down South, I suppose? Maybe you didn't know that he was part of a bunch of men who were involved in just about every kind of crime? You were not aware that his real name is Terrance Kindle and that he ripped off his boss to the tune of a million plus then?"

She gave a little girly gasp evoking in Pitt's mind a scene enacted by Marilyn Monroe in some movie he'd watched recently on TV.

"I had no idea of any of this. Yes, I knew he had money. He invested a sizeable sum in The Green Man but I never asked where he got it from. I sort of guessed that he'd got a bank loan, mortgage or whatever but him a gangster?"

Her voice rose a few octaves at the word 'gangster' She further emphasized her incredulity by shaking her head in disbelief. Pitt ignored what he considered some attempt at the theatrical, shuffled his papers and retrieved another sheet.

"So, the little argument you had outside the church on the day of your husband's funeral with Nial O' Shaughnessy was nothing to do with money and in any case as you've already indicated you have no idea why he might want to attack you?"

Bella King was visibly shaken. She had not been aware that anyone had seen their meeting and was desperately trying to think of a feasible answer.

Pitt continued. "What actually happened Mrs King was that O'Shaughnessy had at last located Terrance Kindle, your husband, and threatened all kinds of nasty things which would happen if you couldn't find the cash. You arranged for the meeting and had young Jones around for protection. How am I doing so far?"

She said nothing and then straightened up in her chair. There was still a hint of defiance in her voice. Any pretence of being the sophisticate was peeled away and she glared at Pitt. The tone was venomous.

"What if it's true what you say? So what! So bloody what! My husband was a total bastard but now I'm rid of him. I mean to keep what I have. Yes, that cockney came demanding money. I had no idea about his role in the city. I thought he was just another of Tom's vile acquaintances, a chancer who thought he'd put one over on the grieving helpless widow. Yes, I had Dean with me. I thought the mere sight of him would cause O'Shaughnessy to turn tail and run but he didn't. He did attack me."

She rolled back a sleeve and revealed a large bruised area on her upper arm.

"I'm sure if I'd been alone, he would have killed me."

"Can you tell me why you kept this from the police? Why would you want to place Dean Jones in a position where he might be either injured or jailed for a long time? We have a strong presence just outside the pub."

Pitt answered his own question.

"Isn't it the case that you had done with the lad, got bored of his constant attention and wanted rid of him?

Wouldn't it be a good idea to rid yourself of two problems all at once? You must have known that O'Shaughnessy was not the nice boy next door and that he was fully intending harm and that having Jones there would result in GBH on one side or the other. The winner gets banged up and the loser is in no fit state to bother you again. Isn't that the real truth of the matter Mrs King?"

Bella King was back in control of the situation. She stretched her arms across the table, hands held palms upwards, a mute plea to be believed. Her beautiful eyes were averted from Pitt's disbelieving gaze. Bella had tried the hardnosed businesswoman and now it was time for her little girl lost persona.

"That's not fair Mr. Pitt. I thought that Dean just being there would be sufficient but it wasn't, was it?"

No, it wasn't thought Pitt and now he would have to continue his previous interview and charge Dean Jones with manslaughter at the very least. The woman was totally amoral and as far as he could understand, Bella and Tom King were a very matched pair indeed.

Chapter 31

"You've gotta see this guv!"

Khunkhun rushed into Pitt's office without the usual formality of knocking on the door and Pitt bawling:

"Come in Jaz!"

The small TV which Pitt had installed ostensibly to keep pace with the latest news was switched on and as the picture came into focus, Pitt was aware of the backdrop of The Green Man. The pub door was opened in the manner of curtains being drawn aside at some West End first night and Bella King stood in the doorway, statuesque as ever. Then after a brief pause, she strode out onto the patio. Pitt could visualise some Nineteen-fifties modelling school with Bella King wandering around balancing half a dozen books on her head and perhaps aiming to be the face of Coco Channel, Revlon, Max Factor or perhaps pictured on the front of 'Vogue'.

The figure was as ever voluptuous, the hair long, raven black and the lips a shade of red exactly matching her shoes. To mark her husband's passing, she wore a hat and veil small enough not to interfere with the general effect of unbridled sensuality.

"Enter the grieving widow Jaz."

Bella struck a pose as a young TV commentator pushed a hand-held microphone into her face. Pitt did not recognise the man. Bella brushed the offending mic to one side better to ensure that the camera produced an unimpeded view of the beautiful but sad face. Then she began. It was a performance that the two officers had been treated to when they had interviewed her. She coughed a little, stumbled over her words, and dabbed at her long eyelashes.

"My husband was a wonderful caring man. He has been taken from me and there must be someone out there who

140

has information that can help the police. I beg you to come forward."

Bella King clasped her hands together as if in prayer and beseeched the millions watching to give her some solace.

"Many in our little community have good reason to be thankful that he joined us here in Egginton. He was a man who tried to give back something to the village; a man who would organise charity events; a man who in the privacy of our home would console the worried. Some have been known to weep on his shoulder in troublesome times."

Bella looked up towards the lowering clouds as if trying to remember happier times.

"Yes, I loved my husband dearly and in the years we were together, there was never a cross word. We would discuss together how we could help in any way when there were problems amongst our guests. He did not think of those enjoying the wonderful atmosphere of The Green Man as a means of earning a living. To him, they were friends; everyone."

She paused and signalled to Tracey the barmaid. Obediently, the latter stepped forward with a glass of water. Bella took a gulp, smiled and glanced upwards towards the brewery's bottle glass windows.

"He was not only a wonderful husband and friend to all but he was dedicated to producing what he claimed was the finest beer in the country and I guess many who have sampled it would not dispute his claim. It was in a place that he loved that he was brutally murdered and once more, I implore whoever did this evil thing to search his or her conscience and come forward."

Bella King slumped forward and was propped up by the ever-watchful Tracey. The effort had drained her mentally and she was led back into The Green Man sobbing theatrically.

"Bloody 'ell boss. What a performance! How soon will King be canonised?"

"Worthy of an Oscar for best actress Jaz. Should go down well on the nationals. Not sure how the locals who actually know what the real setup was between Bella and Tom King will make of that load of bollocks though. Nothing seems to have changed in any way at The Green Man Jaz. I'd have thought that losing Tom King would be like the Miracles losing Smokey Robinson."

"Err who's that guv?"

"Forget it Jaz."

Chapter 32

The Reverend William Milroy, the present incumbent of St. Egbert's Church was perplexed. The current interest in all things Green Man was a little surprising. A great pity that some pre-Christian symbol should evoke a curiosity singularly absent previously with regard to his deeply thought-out sermons. The murder of the leader of the Raggy Men hard on the heels of the macabre death in the brewery had resulted in an unexpected increase in not only Sunday worshippers but also visitors. The village also buzzed with talk of the killing of a London thug. Milroy had experienced a somewhat tightening of his dog collar on overhearing unchristian comments such as: 'Bloody got what 'e deserved I reckon.'

One American with a very large camera and a 'Y'all' Southern accent claimed to be a descendent of some seventeenth-century villager. Everywhere there was a hunger to hear stories and collect memorabilia about The Green Man legend. Still, it did mean more money towards the fund for combating dry rot in the church roof and once the problem of what to do with the colony of protected pipistrelle bats had been sorted out, the work could now commence. The colony of bats in the church roofing resulted in parishioners being subjected to the overpowering stench emanating from large amounts of guano and urine. Nevertheless, the government 'Bat Man' as Reverend Milroy was wont to refer to him had stern facedly pointed out:

'It is illegal to intentionally kill, injure or take any bat or to recklessly damage, destroy or block up their roosts or disturb them'.

Milroy had in a lighter moment remarked that it seemed that God favoured bats rather than the humans he had created in his own image.

The graves had been trampled on; picnic waste discarded around the graveyard and branches had been broken from the yew tree. Names, symbols of all kinds and the inevitable sprayed 'tags' of the so-called graffiti artists were everywhere. Parts of the edge of the slab had been roughly broken off leaving jagged edges. The word 'Resurgam' which not so long ago was almost invisible had now been edged in gold paint so that it stood out boldly from the chaos. The skull engraving had been embellished in red and artistically painted drips of blood had been added. The grass and weeds around the grave had been ground into the mud so that there was now a clarity not afforded to other burials in that part of the cemetery. The warm weather encouraged foraging ants to busy themselves dragging fodder down small holes around the base of the grave.

Reverend Milroy made his way towards The Green Man's grave armed with every kind of cleaning solvent, buckets of water and rags. The weather was fine, the vicar was young and he was not going to allow any part of his graveyard to be left in this way. It was the kind of day when there was no possibility that the grotesquely carved leering gargoyles would be spouting rain water down onto unsuspecting complaining visitors he mused. The Reverend Milroy had taken the precaution of also bringing along a small collapsible metal chair in order to make the chore a little easier to perform. Glancing around and hoping that none of his parishioners would see the leader of the flock in his workaday paint and oil spattered boiler suit garb, he emptied one of his plastic containers onto the surface of the stone. Layers of paint and grime were disappearing surprisingly easily and after about an hour of vigorous rubbing, swilling, and wringing out rags, he was well pleased with his work.

He regarded graveyards as precious places. Deep within the earth the remains of what in life were dreams and hopes fulfilled or unfulfilled; poems and songs thought of but never to be spoken or sung. Yes, the soul had departed but what remained should be respected; even the remains of The Green Man.

In fact, his labours were now giving him an idea for the following Sunday's sermon. He would have something to say about the devil making work for idle hands. Yes St. Paul might kick things off nicely

"We hear that some among you are idle. They are not busy; they are busybodies"

He could sprinkle in a little Proverbs:

"Lazy people irritate their employers, like vinegar to the teeth or smoke in the eyes."

He might finish off with lashings of sloth, one of the deadly sins. Yes, he could really crescendo on that one.

By this time, the sun was high in the sky, bees buzzed, birds chirped and now and then the throaty sound of a frog might be heard coming from the direction of the stream. Milroy was succumbing to the very sloth he had been musing about previously. It was warm, not too hot and one of those hazy days that had the Reverend been holidaying on some far-flung beach, the book he would be reading would have fallen from his hand. He would have dozed safe in the knowledge that the sun cream, lovingly and liberally applied by his wife would protect him from burning. The children would be happily splashing about in the kiddies pool. Yes indeed, the poet Browning might have summed up the day: 'God's in his Heaven. All's right with the world.'

It was at that point that leaning back on the flimsy garden chair, he found himself falling backwards, narrowly escaping having his head connect with a nearby gravestone. He attempted in vain to suppress a curse. Blaspheming on any day of the week was certainly not good practice for one in holy orders. Nevertheless, uncharacteristically for him, he uttered several rather mild oaths which he then tried unsuccessfully to retract due to the possibility of a passing villager hearing his outburst. Milroy extricated himself from the now bent wreckage, brushed himself down, and stared at the hole into which one of the chair's legs was now firmly lodged. He proceeded to retrieve the chair, flinging it to one side. Half-heartedly he flicked soil and grass from his clothes, observing that several grass stains had now been added to the many shades on his boiler suit of many colours.

The hole was small in diameter and loose soil was now falling into what he guessed might be a depth of six inches. His first thought was a rat, rabbit or heaven forefend badger, this latter though highly regarded by animal lovers could create a scarred landscape reminiscent of the fox holes in the First World War. On his customary daily walks, he had seen roadkill on the narrow lanes around Upper Egginton. The teeth on this animal were long and pointy, could inflict a great deal of damage to the unwary and it was therefore with some trepidation that he pushed a broken branch into the hole, fully expecting to be confronted by a set of fangs at the very least. As it was, the only thing moving was a worm wriggling its way back into the depths.

At last, after a brief glance towards the heavens, he adjusted his gardening glove and tentatively felt around in the fissure. At first, there seemed to be nothing and the priest was in the process of coming to the conclusion that the movement of soil and the cracks were a result of erosion through wind, rain and snow around The Green Man's grave. He was about to fill the hole with compost from the decaying pile of flowers situated next to the lichgate when for no obvious reason that he could think of, he plunged his hand once more into the gap. This time he felt something which he guessed was a string or thin twine. He held on to this, pulled, and found himself looking at an old-fashioned oilskin bag about the size of a man's hand. The neck was pulled tight and it took Milroy some time to unravel the twine. Once all was disentangled, he gently pulled on the drawstring. He was about to investigate further but something whispered to him that this was not a situation that he should pursue without police involvement.

His first thought was that of finding a local drug dealer's stash. Hide this in a churchyard? Why not? This would be the last place any policeman would look. Should he open the bag? Definitely not, that from what little he knew, might mean contaminating DNA evidence. The Reverend Milroy was torn between his ever-increasing level of curiosity and a possible admonishment from the local constabulary. Minutes passed but eventually, his inquisitiveness won the day and one further quick pull on the cord holding the neck resulted in a glimpse of bright shining objects hidden within. Further examination exposed a magpie's nest of valuables ranging from pearl and diamond necklaces to diamond-encrusted gold rings. The jewellery was not of modern design. Milroy suspected most were of Victorian or Edwardian origin. He allowed the hoard to cascade through his hands before carefully returning it and closing the neck. This was most definitely a matter for the police. Bluebottles hummed, spiders spun intricate patterns in the undergrowth and Milroy sat bemused, pondering his find.

Chapter 33

A fisherman, staking an early morning claim for his favourite 'peg' on the riverbank spotted the body. It had become trapped against a pier nearest to the riverbank. It lay, face upturned, hair wearing traceries of river sedge grass near the crown whilst longer strands drifted in time with the gentle swirl of the river. One arm rested on the river gravel and shingle used for the pathway. The scene resembled that of a Pre Raphaelite painting, the tragedy of Ophelia by Millais, perhaps, the difference being that this death was no accident. The bank resembled the kind of crime scene familiar to those often shown in TV news bulletins with police officers patrolling and police divers wearing wet suits and breathing apparatus.

The body was brought onto the pathway for Bryn's preliminary examination. The detritus was being carefully removed. Bryn's previous evening had involved consuming ten pints of ale together with whisky chasers. His hangover if measured on the Richter scale might have recorded a nine. Today as with the many boozy nights he had regularly been involved in, his professionalism would in no way be impaired. Pitt greeted him.

"Morning Bryn. Not looking your usual Celtic self."

"I'm fine, fine. Before we start, got a great one for you Pitt"

Pitt made no comment. He sighed impatiently. It was always like this. Over the years he understood that the man's need to block out the sights and senses necessary for his work resulted in a degree of levity which though something he was uncomfortable with, nevertheless tolerated.

"Heard this one last night at our annual reunion. Incidentally, the Port was liquid gold. Marvellous after-dinner speaker. Chap went to the doctor's, had a checkup and asked the doc:

"Do you think I'll live a long and healthy life then?" The doc replied, "I doubt it somehow. Mercury is in Uranus right now."

Fella said, "I don't go in for any of that astrology nonsense."

The doc replied, "Neither do I. My thermometer just broke."

Bryn Edwards hooted with laughter. Pitt rolled his eyes.

Bella King lay still and stiff. Pitt noted that the clothes she was wearing were those she had regarded as suitable for her publican image on their first meeting following the murder of her husband. Bryn pointed to the small neat hole in the forehead. A further bullet had pierced the heart and there was a bloody stain apparent on her once crisp white blouse. The shoe from her right foot was missing.

"Note the entrance wound to the head Pitt. The skin is seared and blackened with what we in the trade call 'powder tattooing'. As you are aware, gunshot wounds inflicted at a distance do not result in this kind of discolouration and the only mark would be where the bullet has pierced the skin. "

"Time of death Bryn?"

Edwards pursed his lips and exhaled.

"Difficult to say. I've no idea how long the body has been in the water and water temperature plays havoc with assessments but my best guess would be say, a little less than twelve hours."

Edwards produced a pair of tweezers from deep within his ancient faded leather satchel. Pitt had never seen the man without his trusty holdall and had often wondered what lay within the inner recesses and what appalling crime scenes it bore witness to. Edwards gestured to the officer, pointing to a safety pin that looked totally out of place on Bella's blouse. On further examination, it was found to have been used to keep a small brown envelope in place within her bra. He unclipped the pin and using the tweezers, gently retrieved the envelope. The sodden, blood-spattered covering was peeled back to reveal a small water-stained card. By the looks of the postmark details, this had been ripped haphazardly from a recently delivered box. The message scrawled upon the cardboard, though smudged was still legible.

"Odd. Very odd Pitt. What the hell does this mean? 'Now you've both paid for what you've done.'"

Bryn Edwards had no explanation.

"If you take whatever the killer is telling us into consideration together with the method of assassination, quite obviously this is no random killing Ben. It is precise, efficient and the perp knew exactly what he or she was doing. The murderer faced the victim at no more than two or three feet. In my opinion and don't take it as gospel; it is only my opinion; the executioner was happy to face the victim eyeball to eyeball. He or she pulled the trigger wishing Bella King to know who was dispatching her. The killing seems to have been completed quickly and without fuss. My first inclination would be to rule out any of the locals in this. I suppose many countryfolk are gun owners but they would have had shotguns or sporting rifles. This looks a bit more Bond-like to me; a Beretta maybe or a similar small handgun presumably with a silencer attachment."

"These days Bryn, there are plenty of illegal guns on the market if you know the right people. You've only to look at the gang related gun death statistics to know that the price of these weapons is within the budget of most and I guess a trip to the city; Brum or Wolverhampton for example might lead to a contact. I don't doubt the opportunity would present itself. I daresay that by now the gun lies deep in Severn River mud."

Chapter 34

Staff and customers at The Green Man were of the opinion that Mrs King was last seen at about eleven forty-five p.m. A couple taking their dog for a late evening walk prior to retiring to bed had waved to Bella as they continued towards their cottage. On leaving the pub, Tracey the barmaid had shouted that she would see her on the following day. In Dean Jones's absence, Bella had herself spent time in the cellar. Mrs King had mentioned to Tracey that she needed to count the empty casks stored at the rear in readiness for an early arrival of draymen the following morning.

"Yes Inspector, she was always like that you know, efficient and that. You gotta be in the pub trade. There's always some bugger ready ter rip yer off."

Tracey was showing signs of tearfulness but determined not to fully show her feelings. It was apparent that in addition to liking the woman, she had the greatest respect for Bella King.

A rash of SOCOs were operating at the rear of The Green Man. Heavy gouts of blood had been found in one area. A track of smears led to the copse of trees bordering the path leading down to the river. It was evident that the killer had dragged Bella King across the cobbles and into the wood. From the extent of blood loss, it seemed likely that she was already dead before being dragged down to the riverbank and pushed into the current.

The draymen had been unaware of any crime. The early morning collection of kegs and crates had resulted in the crime scene being disturbed. The impression made by the lorry tracks mingled with those of private cars, motorcycles and walkers. If the killer had arrived by car, it was in any case, unlikely that he would have parked his vehicle in full view. Pitt theorised that he had made his way up from the Severn through the woods and hidden amongst the containers. If that was the case, he or she might have had a degree of knowledge with regard to Bella King's routine. On the other hand, he did not rule out the possibility that the container store was a first step prior to forcing an entry into The Green Man from the rear. Either way, this did not limit the number of possible perps.

Pitt made his way along the path leading to the river. He looked back at the squat church and straggle of cottages in the distance and then upwards at the now oppressive sky. The summer heat would shortly end with a thunderstorm. Perhaps he might find something which the SOCOs had missed but his aim as ever was to put himself into the mind of whoever had murdered Bella King and dragged her body the few hundred yards to the Severn.

Bushes and nettle beds acted as a natural hedge creating a corridor snaking down towards the water. The police tape was now blowing across the path and winding itself around his ankles. He shook it off and continued on his way. On either side, the undergrowth was alive with movement. Pigeons made their chattering way skyward and a ragged winged large black bird scraped his face as it struggled to exit the brushwood. White butterflies danced and Pitt dodged their crazily choreographed ballet. A loan cowslip still flowered when those around it had long since died away.

The path ended and an ancient, long-abandoned wooden planked landing stage came into view. It had at one time been used by small boats and canoes for pleasure purposes or for fishermen to dangle lines and keep nets. Small spots of blood identical to Bella's blood type had been found on the rotting boards. This then was where she had been brought prior to her corpse being disposed of in the river. Pitt closed his eyes and visualised Bella King's inert body being gently carried along by the waters towards its final resting place at the bridge. The dry reed beds crackled after weeks of sunshine and the river levels were, Pitt noticed, way below the markings on the stone gauge which had long ago been erected to indicate winter and summer heights. In order to launch the body, the killer might have had to step into the mud and reeds. An area of broken vegetation tended to reinforce the theory.

The river sucked and slithered against the ill-defined bank. His eyes were drawn to an empty plastic Evian bottle bobbing up and down trapped in the oily stagnancies marking out the borders of the vegetation. Something else was demanding his attention. The structure on which Pitt stood was unstable and creaking beneath his body weight. He lowered himself and slowly crawling forward along the jetty in order better to view the water below, Pitt saw something red tangled in the river sedge. He made his way back to the bank, broke off a sturdy looking branch from a nearby willow and retraced his steps. He found that he could just about reach the object and after several attempts managed to hook the end of the branch onto it. Pitt had seen this recently. What he held in his hand was one of the red high heeled shoes that Bella King always wore.

In the distance, Pitt could see the smoke from a far away steam train as it made its way along the valley bottom. Families would be enjoying the trip and he could imagine as he himself had done long ago, little children, their fingers writing names on the steamed-up glass windows. This was beautiful, agrarian Shropshire and not some rotting high rise council estate where junkies regularly stabbed junkies, gangs shot members of competing gangs or where women were battered to death by drunken partners. These two worlds were now in conjunction. In this small area of what had been designated as of outstanding natural beauty, four murders had taken place within a period of a few weeks.

Chapter 35

With some effort, he pushed his way past the unsuspecting policeman, rudely interrupting his afternoon 'fag break'. Unhindered, he hurried on towards the closed cabin door. The kick did not damage it seriously but was sufficient to open it. It had not in any case been locked. He felt a wave of satisfaction flood over him. If you can't kick the law, then kick its door he mused.

Pitt and Khunkhun had been involved in a mundane filing exercise. To be more precise Khunkhun filed, Pitt advised. The mounds were piling up and it was necessary to keep some kind of order now that the files were about to be transferred to the Wolverhampton H. Q. Andy Jones interrupted the matter in hand.

"Right here I am. Best to get in 'ere myself before you send some bugger out to bring me in the back of a panda car. You can't 'ave my brother for it so yer bound to 'ave me. Am I right?"

Pitt did not look up but responded,

"I guess from what you say that you have something to tell us about Mrs King's murder. You had plenty to say about the lady last time we met so you are correct in your assumption that we shall be interviewing you as to your whereabouts on the night of her death. We shall be interviewing all who were in The Green Man on that same night. Should you wish to make a statement whilst you are here without a solicitor that is your choice. We're moving back to the city over the next few days so unless you want a trip over there, it's in your interest to make yourself available as soon as possible."

"Ave me come to you lot in Wolverhampton? You'd love that wouldn't you? Dragging me away from a day's money so you can do yer paperwork?"

"Let's get to the point shall we Mr Jones. Do you wish to make some kind of statement? If so, perhaps you could follow DS Khunkhun into the rear of the cabin, settle yourself down and allow him to take your statement."

Under his breath, Pitt whispered,

"And if not, stop wasting my time!"

"Mmmm I see, bloody beneath you to deal with me directly. Gotta pass it on to this one 'ave we? What's 'e then? The 'ouse Paki?"

Pitt's eyes blazed. The papers he had been carefully placing into separate piles were swept from the desk and in an instant, he had Jones pinned against the wall, both hands holding his lapels. The men were of a similar height and weight but at that moment, Pitt seemed to rise up above the man, his barrel shaped chest heaving with anger. He kicked aside a glass paperweight that had fallen to the floor.

"You little racist shit! I'm not about to discuss this with you. Get into the back room, treat the DS with some respect and then maybe I won't break your arm. Then you can go back to poaching rabbits, mugging old ladies, or whatever….. You don't know me but believe it, I'm not averse to just a tiny wee bit of police brutality when I have to deal with bastards like you."

Pitt, maintaining hold of his coat, frog marched Jones backwards through the dividing doorway and into the office to the rear. Jones did not retaliate. Khunkhun could hear the sound of tearing fabric. By the time Jaz had followed Pitt into the room, Andy Jones was sitting or rather was slumped on an office chair, meek and mild as a scolded five-year-old who has just refused his broccoli. He remained motionless, head down. Jaz smiled; now here was a clear case of a gaffer induced post-traumatic stress disorder. Pitt winked, brushed past him and returned to his paperwork. He could partially hear Khunkhun's questioning through the partitioning wall and Jones's mumbled responses. Andy Jones was cooperating. After a few hours, Pitt heard the door at the rear of the cabin being slammed to. Khunkhun joined him.

"It seems that went well then Jaz?"

"Very much so guv. I think he was well impressed with your 'bad cop' act. To cut it short, Jones was in The Green Man until closing time but kept his drinking to a minimum. He reckons he was on a promise from one of the young ladies. I've got the details and I'll be checking it out with her later. She went early he says to err, prepare things at her flat if you get my drift. He left the pub and went back to his lodgings to; 'freshen up' and change his clothes. Then it was off to a midnight soiree which ended at about ten the following morning. No one was up at his lodgings. He has his own key so for the hours in question we have no proof of his comings or goings. He admits he'd have liked to have done for Mrs King but to be honest guv, I really don't think he's got the balls for it. I guess you may have had the same idea earlier on. The man's all mouth and trousers. Oh, and by the way, thanks for dealing with him. I was just about to deck him and find myself reduced to directing traffic."

Pitt nodded his agreement.

"Yes, I see him as a small-time chancer Jaz but definitely not a killer and certainly not a man to carry it out in such a cold-blooded way. Nevertheless, as you say, his amorous evening still needs checking out. It's not urgent and it can be done once we've transferred back to the city. In any case, looking through this lot, there's still one of the Morris dancers to interview."

Chapter 36

Khunkhun walked towards the mish-mash of farm buildings. He was hot and sticky and his shirt was plastered to his back. He really could do without this one he thought. Pretty stupid of him not to take Stan Till's statement whilst he was in the village but at the time he had felt nothing but pity for this wheelchair-bound veteran. The man was still inconsolable after the death of his sister. That day in the churchyard had really not been the time or the place.

He caught a whiff of fragrance from the old English lavender growing leggy and untended in a small herb garden. Judging by the number of buildings, at some time this must have been a thriving smallholding. That was long ago and all had been abandoned bar for the farmhouse, freshly painted and with a new roof, standing out like a single white polished tooth in a mouthful of rotting teeth. He walked past what was once a thriving orchard. Those same trees were now lichen covered, ragged specimens. In the absence of any pruning or spraying against infestation, they produced small maggot filled apples that lay in abundance around the roots. Wasps feasted greedily, swooping down to feed then rising to hover above the decaying fruit. The oak timbered front door was large and gave the impression of this Englishman's home undoubtedly being his castle. Khunkhun noticed a ramp had been installed to facilitate Till's wheelchair access. A large brass ship's bell had been attached to the wall. He tugged at the knotted cord attached to a cast iron ringer. The effect was immediate; the noise echoing across the area. Khunkhun shuffled his feet impatiently but no sound came from within the house.

From somewhere within one of the dilapidated outbuildings a voice shouted,

"I'm in here."

He made his way in the general direction, checking each shed and barn as he went until he came to what might once have been a lockable area where tractors, harvesters and expensive farm equipment might have been stored. Stan Till was holding on to a wheelchair with one hand whilst in the other he held an oily rag which he was using to clean what Khunkhun recognised as a Nineteen-Sixties Triumph Tiger Cub. He had seen old photos of one belonging to his father. The latter had been the proud owner prior to his wedding but had sold it to pay for the nuptials. He would often extol the virtues of the machine to his son

"200 ccs; single cylinder; rear swinging-arm with twin suspension units Jaz. What a machine that was! Painted the petrol tank on mine red."

He noted that Stan Till's machine was the original silver.

"She's a beauty Mr Till" he said. "My old man would be in motorcycling Heaven looking at that."

Till looked up from his work, threw the rag to one side and eased himself gently back into his wheelchair.

"Yes, but some bloody use to an old crock like me. Still, I keep it shined and in tip-top condition just in case you know. Miracles sometimes happen. Bought it when I was seventeen. I used to race it along the road from Bridgnorth to Wolverhampton. Dangerous stretch that. At least a couple of racers die every year. Deceptive yer see. All of a sudden, you're off a straight and on to a sharp bend. Mmm, treacherous. Anyway, enough of my reminiscences. What can I do for you Mr err Khunkhun was it?"

"You seem to have a good head for names sir. Yes, let's talk. Call me Jaz."

"Probably more comfortable in the house Jaz. Just let me do my three-point turn in this bloody contraption and we can sit and have a cuppa."

The sound of his chair reverberated across the cobbles throwing up detritus as it rumbled on its way. Somewhere far off a wood fire was burning. Jaz could taste the smoke. Once up the ramp, Till produced a key attached to a necklace of string from beneath his shirt and opened the door. Khunkhun followed him several steps behind. Till was half lifting himself to press several switches on a panel. The light revealed a hallway that screamed beige. The polished parquet floor was redolent of times long gone. Stan Till manoeuvred himself around the doorway leading into a clean functional living room. Khunkhun observed that the furniture, though dated was spotless and placed in a way to give maximum space for Till and his chair. Surprisingly, in the fireplace, a bunch of fresh red roses had been placed in a flower-decorated vase, not the kind of thing one might expect from a crippled ex squaddie. Till had noted his reaction.

"Not my doing Jaz. I have a cleaning lady in once a week."

He swept a hand around to indicate the bright clean aspect.

"Not a spot of dust anywhere. As you can see, she does a great job. I just need to keep things spick and span between visits. Difficult with the chair and all but it tends to come naturally to someone brought up in the Forces. I'm really proud of the tight corners on my bed linen."

He chuckled an earthy chuckle

Khunkhun sat in a comfortable armchair and declined the coffee offered by Till from a large thermos flask.

"I make it in the morning and it serves me all day. Saves me the effort of going in and out of the kitchen. I do the same with my sandwiches."

He pointed to a plastic container on a coffee table.

"I guess you want a statement from me to complete your records? I don't think it will help you much but well it's the usual bloody paperwork to keep the box tickers happy."

Khunkhun produced a biro and a sheaf of headed notepaper attached to a clipboard and passed these over to Till.

"I'd like two statements please Mr Till; one for the day of Mr King's murder and another for the night in The Green Man before Mrs King was killed. I'm told that all the Raggy Men were drinking in there till closing time?"

"That is true but I don't think that in either case what I put down will be of interest but nevertheless....."

Till scratched his head, giving the impression that he was trying to recover images of the times specified. Then he was writing, stopping now and then to recap on what he had written. Khunkhun had explained that any mistakes should be crossed through and initialled. Till signed and extracted the first sheet before passing it to the officer.

"I think that's about all I can remember about King's death. No great loss but perhaps I shouldn't say that."

Without waiting for a reply, he turned back to the clipboard and began to write what he knew about the evening session in The Green Man prior to Bella King's murder. Half an hour later Khunkhun was in possession of two statements signed by Till.

Till said wistfully; "She looked particularly glamorous that night. I remember one of the Raggy's trying it on with her, in an innocent way you know. Made a comment about those red stilettos. I hear you coppers found one in the reeds on the river bank. Must have lost it as she was being thrown in. All very sad and a big loss to the local community."

"You may be right Mr Till but investigations are ongoing and I can't comment of course."

Till touched the side of his nose and smiled.

"I understand. Hush, hush, Official Secrets Act and all that."

Khunkhun thanked the man and made an excuse to leave. There was plenty of work still to be done.

Chapter 37

They were packed into the cliff railway's single carriage. The Nineteen-Fifties aluminium cars crossed halfway along the two hundred feet of track leading up the crag from Low Town to High Town. Passengers in the descending cab had moved across to get a better view and wave excitedly at the dancers. The Raggy Men were on their way to the Bridgnorth Pageant. Their leader was dead but at a hastily-convened meeting in The Green Man, it was agreed that they perform nevertheless and dedicate their efforts to him. Old enmities were in evidence prior to alighting. There had been sullen faces and glares between dancers from the moment they had assembled on the village green prior to moving off in convoy to Low Town. The atmosphere within the confines of the cab for its short cliff journey was poisonous beyond belief. The crush within the tiny vehicle produced a wave of sweaty anger. All were aware of what they would describe as 'dirty linen' being washed in the public glare. There had been incessant arguments when the contents of police statements became known as each member was interviewed and made aware of what others had reported.

The group lined up waiting for the doors to open. Then in angry silence, they pushed and jostled their way out onto the castle ramparts. They made their way past the historic remains of the castle destroyed during the Civil War. The walls still strained bravely to avoid collapse and had managed for centuries to perch proudly at an alarming angle, a relic of conflicts unknown by many. They danced and jingled onto the High Street, heading towards the old Town Hall. The building had been a landmark since the 17th Century and had been the centre of the town's civic & legal affairs. That was long ago and today beneath its oak framed pillars, instead of the local market, it would ring to laughter and applause as the pageant's procession moved slowly along the street. The sun shone down kindly on all taking part and the hall's beautiful stained-glass windows seemed to be shining with pride for the town and its citizens.

This was one high street that was not ravaged by on line shopping. People came from all over the country and from far off lands to savour the beauty and absorb the centuries of history that had gone into creating this unique environment. Eras came and went but here in a part of Shropshire, the best of the old was preserved. The Raggy Men's dancing shoes clattered on the cobbles as they followed on behind the many floats. Here was the farmers' float with members of the local Young Farmers' Association dressed up in smocks and carrying imitation scythes. There was the Miss Shropshire float with Miss Shropshire waving, queen-like whilst her attendants, Miss Bridgnorth and Miss Stourport sat demurely at her feet.

An expensively dressed middle-aged woman walked her labradoodle determinedly ignoring the entertainment. The animal halted and without warning, squatted and deposited a dollop of excrement onto the footpath, the result of that morning's hearty canine breakfast of half a tin of Pedigree Chum. The woman, her face giving the impression that a regular daily injection of Botox ensured that she could avoid even the subtlest of smiles, retrieved a small wet-looking mop from within a black poo bag. After removing the offensive mound and tying the bulging bag in a knot, she gently cleaned the pavement and continued on her way.

The watching officers were well away from the general crowd, standing in the doorway of Beaman's Butchers, gorging themselves on Beaman's Cornish Pasties. They could see without being seen.

"Looks like the locals keep their town clean guv and hey this is some parade they've organised!"

DCI Ben Pitt was reading the leaflet handed to him by an organiser.

"Says here that the town's had a chequered history Jaz. A Norman baron gouging out the eyes of his enemy and Charles the First praising the place. I guess that was before the Parliamentarians knocked it about a bit. Then to cap it all, Hitler had plans to make the place the English equivalent of The Wolf's Lair."

"More like The Badger's Set around here I'd have thought guv."

A young woman passed them pushing a baby buggy. Pitt nodded towards a section of the crowd some twenty yards down the High Street on the opposite side. Joe Palin and his wife were staring intently at the dancers as they passed. The expression on his face made it clear that he had no truck with any of them. They did not accept him within their tight-knit group and he couldn't stand those bloody stuck-up bastards but it was a day out so he'd be on his best behaviour.

The Raggy Men were coming to the end of their routine. Stan Till had ceased to gyrate in and out with his wheelchair and was heading further up the street and onto the disabled ramp leading into the local Wetherspoons. Sticks clashed in time with the accordion then suddenly, chaos reigned. The Raggy Men ceased their dancing as Jakey James aimed a fearsome blow at Peter Jackman, missed and ended up floundering on his back. The melee was brief but attracted far more interest than the dances which had preceded it. Mobile phones flashed; there was a ripple of cynical applause and then the rest of the Raggy Men closed in and parted the pair.

"Should we intervene sir?"

"Definitely not Jaz. Let's see what comes out of this little party piece first."

Round Jakey James was up and bellowing. His mane of long hair cascaded down his back as he pointed furiously at Jackman with his stick.

"You fuckin bastard! You tried to get the cops onto me din't yer. Told 'em I might 'ave done Jim in over money. Told 'em I was followin 'im daint yer. I might be skint but I aint that bloody skint. You tryin to take the heat offen yerself are yer?"

Peter Jackman said nothing, opened his arms wide in an exaggerated gesture of amazement, shrugged and walked away.

"Is this the last of The Raggy Men do you think guv?"

Pitt did not reply.

Chapter 38

The watcher lay in the long quitch grass just outside the outer limits of the wood. All around him moths flittered upwards towards the stars. He had taken up his position stealthily. There was no street lighting to give away his presence and he would not act until he was certain the building was completely empty. He had no hatred for those who were acting as custodians. The sign on the door read 'Closed until further notice, sadly due to death of the proprietor.' He combed the exterior with his binoculars. There were no signs of life. She had switched off the internal lights when she had left and he was pleased to see that the upper floor sash window was still lowered presumably to air the rooms or maybe due to an oversight.

The man had been very careful with the purchase of the drone, especially regarding the explosives. If you had the money, he had found that there was always someone willing to supply. He surveyed the building once more. It was important that the final part of his mission be completed; then and only then could he once more return to a normal life. The drone had been expensive, an internet purchase. He insisted upon the very latest technology. It was imported from the USA and even though he felt that he had covered his tracks, it was his intention that once used; he would ditch it into the River Severn.

He had recognised Tracey in the half-light as she locked the front door. He had no idea who had given her the responsibility for the pub or maybe she had just taken it upon herself to ensure that all was well. An empty pub was fertile ground for any thief. The drone was prepared and ready. He would pilot this using camera and a hand-held transmitter to remotely control the machine. The 'copter was rising with just the sound of the rotors to disturb the cooling evening darkness. It rose high enough to be silhouetted, *'E.T'* -.*like* against the fullness of the silver moon. The explosives were attached firmly and the timer had been set for thirty minutes giving him enough time to disappear into the woods and be far enough away before the blast. There were enough plastics for him to both hear and see the effect. He smiled contentedly.

The drone had now reached its destination. He moved the right stick into a hover position and then came the most difficult part of the operation. The manoeuvre involved presenting the drone before the opening, releasing the micro catches and tilting the machine so that its payload slid through the open window; difficult but not impossible and something well prepared for during his test flights.

He pushed the right stick forwards ever so gradually. The payload began to slide. He could not be certain whether the plastics would end up within the bedroom or fall to the ground. He calculated that the latter would merely be a win situation whilst the former would be a win, win, win. It took almost a minute and then to his joy the load slid silently into the room. He was forced to stifle a shout of sheer elation as he manoeuvred the drone away and piloted it above his head towards the river. He was close enough to the river bank to ensure that the dropping point would be midstream where the Severn was at its deepest. He throttled the machine down reducing the height gradually until it finally slid beneath the waters.

He wriggled backwards on his belly into the woodland. Once out of sight, he could stand with impunity and make his way down to the path alongside the river. When it came, even as far away as he was, the noise was deafening and he could see a huge plume of fire in the distance. The Green Man was no more; he had consigned its vile legacy to the place in hell that it warranted. All around him waterfowl sped up in alarm. His mission was finally ended as he had hoped it would.

Chapter 39

As he was wont to say, Pitt had a 'feeling in his buttocks' that there was something staring him in the face that he had missed. He had dispensed with his tie and unbuttoned his shirt collar. The windows in his office had been flung wide open. On another day, the ancient stays holding them would have rattled on their catches. His shirt, freshly extracted from its cellophane wrapping and still bearing the newness of horizontal and vertical creases was patterned with tidemarks of sweat. The thought crossed his mind that he might be gently frying in the intense heat. The last time he had felt so uncomfortable had been on a holiday to Fuerteventura. Even in that heat, at least there had been the cooling gusts. He had often watched international windsurfers waiting to take advantage of the conditions. Now and then, the stillness was disturbed by passing traffic. The sound was as though some giant insect had buzzed its way towards the window and then retreated. Any discernible draft and the resulting gentle rippling was not sufficient to disturb the carefully placed papers.

Pitt had spread the contents across his desk. Though no expert on valuing antique jewellery, he was by no means ignorant in such matters. He had for many years watched TV programs where similar items were valued. His favourite was *'The Antiques Road Show'* and with the amateur knowledge he had gained he made a guess that what he was looking at was at the very least worth half a million pounds. It was yet to be verified but he had no doubt that this was what remained of Terrance Kindle, (aka Tom King's) haul. Nial O'Shaughnessy would never know how close he had been to his mother's gems. The contretemps Pitt had witnessed in the church's car park between O'Shaughnessy and Bella King had occurred no more than fifty yards away from the find. For once, Pitt could see no involvement of Bella King. Her husband had buried the haul in what in retrospect was the most obvious of places, the grave of The Green Man. Under normal circumstances, the resting place would be overgrown with weeds but the publicity resulting from King's death had meant quite the opposite of what had been intended.

Bella King's murder had added to the already Gordian Knott of what he had found to be an altogether intractable problem. He could see motives for the husband and wife's murders but as to any linkage with Jim Walsh's killing? Nothing! There were spreadsheets and all manner of computer readouts but it would be old-style police work that was needed now to make sense of the page after page of information most of which was irrelevant. The reams of statements provided by staff needed to be consolidated, reduced to basics and put in some kind of order. He had long ago perfected a personal version of group 'brainstorming' where he would quickly scribble down significant information about a case and later, cherry pick and create a series of salient 'bullet points'. He noted:

There is a connection in the case between members of a Morris dance group known as The Raggy Men. Two of their number had been murdered. The first victim was the publican and brewer, real name, Terrance Kindle who had assumed the name of Tom King on moving North. The other victim was Jim Walsh, the leader of the group. King was a known associate of a London villain and had made Upper Egginton his base in order to ensure anonymity. Walsh was a solid citizen of some standing in the community. Bella and Tom King's murders were obviously related but not so Walsh's.

There was the investment in land around The Green Man which could pay off handsomely. Raggy Investments Ltd, the company set up for this purpose had been investigated by Khunkhun. The major shareholders were Tom King, Bella King and Peter Jackman. Minor investments were held by other group members. All the shareholders bar Tom King had voted to sell off the land at a substantial profit. King, as the majority shareholder had blocked this. In addition, Jackman was in hoc to Jim Walsh to the tune of seventy thousand pounds at five per cent interest. The loan repayment was due and Jackman's finances were in a dire state. Jakey James also had financial problems. The real enigma though was the destruction of The Green Man pub. What on earth would be the motive for that unless maybe it might speed up the sale of land to developers but surely the risk involved far outweighed this?

King's dalliances with women he had used would make him the target for husbands or maybe even wives. Joe Palin was possibly a suspect for Tom King's murder. He had motive and uncontrolled anger but he was not the kind of man to kill King in such a bizarre fashion. His method would have been to empty the contents of his shotgun into King's head. Although adored by many of the female customers, Pitt felt that at the same time, there was a general undercurrent of hatred for Tom King. It could just have been a killing unconnected with others but the odds for that were incredibly long and Pitt had dismissed this.

Why were all three murders carried out in a different manner? Both King and Walsh had suffered head trauma but King had been displayed macabrely and theatrically. A great deal of imagination and planning must have been involved. Bella King on the other hand had been killed efficiently and professionally by gunshot and an as yet meaningless message had been attached to the body. The use of plural on the message: 'Now you've both paid for what you've done.' might indicate that both King murders were carried out for the same reason but how did that explain Walsh's murder?

Pitt read and reread the statements and after a while, his mind drifted back to Bella King's remains draped lifelessly on the riverbank fully clothed apart from a missing red shoe. There was something on the outer edges of his thought, nibbling away, desperate to make contact.

It was that kind of intuition that Pitt had never dismissed as fantasy. To him, intuition was in the nature of some deeply buried truth trying to find its way into his consciousness. Then it came to him. He flicked through the statements until he arrived at the one he had been searching for. His finger moved down the document, slowly at first and then faster. It was a note by Khunkhun stapled to one of the statements.

Chapter 40

"Who else knew where I had found the shoe Jaz?"

"As far as I know guv, it was you, me and the SOCOs. Even the SOCOs did not know exactly where. They guessed it was in the river but that's about it. The Press just reported that we'd found the other shoe and not the location. He could have made an intelligent guess though."

"What you reported that he actually said was far too specific to be just guesswork Jaz. He talks about finding the shoe in the reed bed. How would he have known with that degree of accuracy where it turned up?"

"Maybe some local gossip saw you down there boss. You know what things are like in tight local communities."

"I can assure you that I was completely alone down at the jetty Jaz. Almost poetic it was. The river, the birds, the trees and me."

"The bloke's an invalid. He spends his time trolling around in a wheelchair guv. There's no connection, no motive, nothing."

"I agree that he's just about the most unlikely villain Jaz but my copper's nose is beginning to smell that something just isn't right with Mr Till. Give him a tinkle, will you? On second thoughts we'll just turn up uninvited. You never can tell what we might find when he's not on his guard."

Khunkhun shrugged his shoulders. Bloody waste of time and effort he thought. Still, he's the boss.

They arrived sometime during the afternoon, parked the car a quarter of a mile down the road from Till's cottage and proceeded to walk the rest of the way. Stan Till would be totally unprepared for the arrival of the two officers. Khunkhun had spent most of the journey mumbling his disquiet about treating a war hero in such a way.

The officers made their way along the path leading through the ruined farm buildings and on towards the cottage. They were at pains not to give any warning of their passage whilst at the same time not wishing to give the impression that they were anything other than policemen on a routine visit. No words passed between them and Khunkhun indicated the direction by hand signals only. They moved around the exterior expecting any moment to see Till but all was silent. Then suddenly they heard the roar of a machine coming from somewhere amongst the barns. They strode briskly in the direction of the noise, past the orchard brushing away wasps and flies hovering in their path. As they came closer, Pitt indicated that they slow down and once more tread gently as they approached the barn where Khunkhun had met Stan Till on his previous visit.

Rather than entering directly, they made their way down the side of the building. All but one window had been boarded over and Pitt sidled towards it. Using his jacket covered arms; he pushed aside the abundance of nettles and wherever possible, crushed the weeds beneath his feet. The ivy which blanketed the window with its greenery now totally covered one side of the building and its tendrils were clawing ever upwards towards the roof. Pitt gently pulled aside the ivy curtain, coughed as the years of dust was dislodged and rubbed away the filth. Inside, finger-thick cobwebs obscured the view but nevertheless, the officer could make out enough to satisfy the theory that had been morphing in his brain for the last few hours. He motioned to Khunkhun .

Stan Till was dressed in worn blue overalls. He sat astride his Triumph Tiger Cub motor bike, back ramrod stiff, head and shoulders perfectly positioned. He had turned the machine off, then looking thoughtfully at the bike, he once more kick-started the engine. Blue smoke was emitted from the exhaust pipe. Having tested the running, Till grasped the hand throttle, and with a twist of his wrist, once more turned the motor off. He gave a satisfied nod of the head, then after glancing upwards, alighted and with easy strides made his way towards a section of metal shelving. This was attached against the wooden wall to a height of perhaps fifteen or so feet and it was necessary to drag over a heavy-looking ladder, lift and place it against the wall. He tested for stability and then began to climb. After a moment or two's searching, he reached for a can of what the officers assumed was engine oil and then began his descent. Pitt whispered;

"Jesus saith unto him; rise, take up thy bed and walk'. The man's no more disabled than I am Jaz."

Khunkhun was at first amazed then angry at what was before him. The man was a complete fraud but why would a perfectly able-bodied man wish to give the impression of disability necessitating a wheelchair? Pitt put a warning finger to his lips signalling that the pair should maintain silence. He led the way back towards the double doors, waited a moment and then shouted,

"Mr Till, are you in there? Could we have a moment of your time please? DCI Pitt and DS Khunkhun here on police business."

The officers could hear a rustling from within; Till was returning to his wheelchair and preparing to adopt his battle-weary character.

"They're unlocked, just give them a tug."

Khunkhun swung open the doors. Till was shielding his eyes from the shaft of sunlight.

"Come on in, I'm just playing about with my favourite lady. Come and have a look at her."

Though stained with black patches of oil, there was a smooth section of flooring leading from the entrance which served perfectly to enable Till to move the wheelchair. He swung it around and swung around and glided towards the motorbike. The officers followed, saying nothing. The bike was indeed a beauty and would still stand out if compared to its Twenty-first Century high tech offspring. Pitt ran his finger along the petrol tank and looked down at the kick starter pedal.

"It must have been something of an effort to get the engine running Mr Till."

Till hesitated then smiled.

"Luckily, I've still got a bit of use in my right leg and I usually put the old iron on it just in case when I'm messing about in here. "

He revealed a metallic looking support cage extending from ankle upwards and past his knee. You are good, very good thought Pitt but not good enough you murderous bastard.

"I have a few questions for you that need clearing up."

Till made as if to adjust himself to a more comfortable position in his wheelchair. He had positioned himself next to the Tiger Cub. His hand was casually draped across the petrol tank. He looked relaxed.

"Carry on Inspector. I'm only too happy to help."

"Well, you see Mr Till, I have something of a conundrum to work out here. Bella King had a particularly noticeable pair of red shoes. She wore them several times when we interviewed her and she was wearing them the night she was murdered."

Till stretched, flicked an imaginary smut of oil from the tank and looked Pitt straight in the face.

"Yes, I have seen them. I guess every male in the village noticed them. Damn great high stilettos. A bit tarty I thought. So where is this leading?"

Pitt feigned a further examination of the motor bike, and without looking up at Till replied,

"What we need to know is how you knew that one of the shoes was found next to the landing stage on the Severn and to be more accurate, in the reeds alongside. I came across it purely by luck and we deliberately kept the details of this from the Press. So how were you to know Mr Till?"

The silence that followed was broken only by the rustling of animals in the undergrowth surrounding the barn or the far off calls of birds. Till was analysing his position and constructing a suitable answer. When it came, it was weak and implausible.

"I guess one of your technical blokes must have let it out over a pint in The Green Man inspector. Word gets around and I must have overheard something. "

"The shoe was placed in an evidence bag and only then did any of the SOCOs know I had found it. As to the positioning, only I and DS Khunkhun were aware as to precisely where it was found. The other problem we have Mr Till is how a paraplegic can suddenly climb a ladder. That really is a conundrum which you might also be able to explain to us?"

Chapter 41

Without warning, Till cast aside his wheelchair and showing amazing agility was astride the Tiger Cub and had kicked the machine into roaring action before the officers could react. He sped the motorcycle towards the open frontage. Pitt was shouting into his mobile radio as he ran, gasping out a message that all roads out of Upper Egginton should be closed off and giving a description of Till and his machine. He was aware that this might be of little avail since Till could head across country. He visualised a kind of Steve McQueen chase as in a scene from the film, *The Great Escape.* Pitt was first to reach the car. Once his fellow officer was installed in the passenger seat, he gunned the car along the narrow lane.

The DCI concentrated on his driving whilst Khunkhun fiddled with the car's police radio. Reception was poor but a degree of communication proved possible. Till had been spotted heading towards Bridgnorth. A patrol car that had blocked the road had proved to be insufficient to prevent his escape but the officer reporting in assured Pitt that a two-car roadblock was now in place at a narrow strip of the road as it twisted its way close to the river. Should Till avoid this, a spike strip had been put in position some yards beyond. It was hoped that the weapon would not need to be used as the resulting punctures at the speed Till was travelling, together with his lack of head protection could result in a fatality.

The roadblock was in place. Pitt now learned that a couple of motorcycle cops had been despatched from Bridgnorth and might arrive at the scene at about the same time as Till. Through the static, the officers heard the voice of the senior policeman bawling out;

"There he is, cut him off!" followed by; "My God he's heading down the path towards the river. He'll not be able to stop......................He's in!"

There was no further clear communication, just a continuation of cross talk and babble interspersed with crackle. When at last Pitt and Khunkhun arrived on the scene, officers were scurrying to and fro through the wooded area, they could see men pointing towards the river. Pitt did not know the man in charge. He showed his warrant card as the officer approached, gasping and white-faced.

"There was nothing we could do sir. He was like a lunatic. He came at us screaming some obscenity, veered off and as soon as he saw the police bikes, headed for the water. There's a ten feet drop. He just went at it like a stunt man; in the air and then down. There's no sign of him sir. I guess that's it. The current's strong there. You'd never swim out of that."

Khunkhun's thoughts returned to his interview with Till.

"I was once a sergeant and now I'm a bloody useless cripple. To look at me now, you wouldn't believe I was once the Brigade's swimming champion. Hell, I once did a sponsored Channel swim."

He turned to Pitt.

"That's as maybe guv but I still think we should have men searching the bank. Till was once a more than adequate swimmer."

Chapter 42

Pitt and Khunkhun sat in Till's front room. Pitt instructed the officer to lever off the padlock and chain on the metal box found in the search of the property. Inside was a tape recorder circa mid-Seventies. A tape had been left inside the machine. Pitt gently lifted out the recorder and plugged it into the nearest socket. There was also a pad containing several pages of neat closely written script. The DCI signalled to the constable that he was no longer required and suggested he make himself a cuppa in Till's kitchen. Once he had closed the door, Pitt pressed the rewind button and when this was completed, both detectives sat back in the armchairs to listen.

It was a female voice, young and so quietly spoken that it was necessary to turn up the volume to the maximum. The reader punctuated her communication with sobs and the occasional gasping for air.

'Dearest Stan, by the time you hear this, I shall be long gone. I have made up my mind. I can see no other way through it. I know this will cause you great grief and I am sorry for that but things are now at a stage where I just can't go on. I think you deserve to know why the seventeen-year-old girl you knew would want to end her life.

It started with my first experience of real love for a man. The passion I felt for Tom was overpowering and all else was blanked out of my life. I gave him all my love and he responded in kind or so I thought. We were so happy for almost six months and when I told him about the child, I thought he too would be as ecstatic as I was. The scan showed the baby was a little girl.

I cannot explain the devastation I felt when his love turned to anger and a fierce hatred of me. You brought me up and gave me all the love you had after our parents died so I had never really experienced anything like it before. He gave me money for an abortion and a card giving the whereabouts of the nearest clinic. I just could not believe this was happening.

I had no idea where to turn but eventually, I decided that I should speak to Bella. I did not think she had known about our affair but as it was her husband's child, I thought she might advise me. She seemed very kind and understanding but also told me that I should 'get rid' of the child. I told her that I could not think clearly since speaking to Tom and I had slept only intermittently. She gave me a full box of her sleeping tablets and told me to use them as needed. I cannot tell whether she knew I would use them as I now intend. I can see no other way out of this.

You will always have my love and gratitude. Goodbye for now dear brother. Love, Alice.'

The officers could hear the sound of kisses followed by sobs and then the tape ended. Pitt flicked off the play button and turned to the letter.

Chapter 43

'To whoever finds this, may I explain the reasons for my actions:

Pitt read the letter out loud:

"My injuries were thought to be permanent and that it was inevitable that I would spend the rest of my life either bedridden or in a wheelchair. In my own mind, I felt that I could overcome my disabilities. In those days of not so long ago, I felt I could prevail over just about anything that was put before me and I thank the Army for giving me that kind of mindset. I had received a very disturbing letter from Alice at this time and it was apparent that she needed me far more than 'Queen and Country'. She did not make it clear in her letter what the problem was but the tone gave me serious grounds for concern. I am therefore ashamed to say that I hid my recovery from those excellent people at the Queen Elizabeth Hospital in Birmingham and was duly invalided out of the army with a pension. Recovery would have meant another two years to complete my term.

Not even Alice knew that I was back in the country. I guess had there been a meeting in the possible glare of publicity; I would not have been able to maintain my charade when faced with her tears at the sight of me in a wheelchair. I look back now and think; 'if only'. If only I had been there for her. As it was, I received news of her suicide just a few days before the end of my stay in hospital. The news was kept from me alas on doctor's orders for fear of a relapse so convincing had been my acting.

I came back to the village and made my home here to be near her. It was only then that I found her tape and only God knows my reaction to what I heard. The weight of the burden over my inability to have prevented her death or to take revenge grew steadily more impossible to bear. I sank into deep despair. I could neither eat nor sleep and indeed I contemplated taking my own life. I believe that I must have been close to insanity at that time. Then almost as though a switch had been thrown in my fevered brain, I knew what had to be done and that all else must be subservient to this one course of action. Someone had to pay and that someone was Tom King. At that point Bella King, though also in some way responsible would be allowed to live. It was only after seeing her television interview that I knew she too had to die and that the whole stinking cesspit that was The Green Man must also be wiped from the face of the earth.

King was easy. You will be aware that The Green Man is part of a terrace. I made my way into the garden of the derelict end terrace property and hid my chair. I had previously unscrewed the fixings and replacing them on my return was a simple matter. No one saw me.... Once we had finished dancing, I made my way into the garden of the derelict end terrace property. No one saw me and had I been spotted; I would have a story ready.

"Oh, I'm inspecting the property with a view to buying."

As it was, everyone was involved in the Fun Day. I had known of the interlinking roof space leading to The Green Man ever since as a boy I had played with one of the children from the cottages. We used to fool around up in the loft and when we were feeling adventurous, crawl along the terrace's roof space playing a kind of game of 'chicken'. There were many times when we came close to falling through the ceilings.

It's pretty easy to disable a man, even one as strong as King if you've had the right training. He was in any case so involved with his precious beer that he was unaware of me climbing into the brewery. I had secreted a length of knotted rope in the wheelchair's shopping bag and brought it with me into the loft space. I attached this to a stanchion, opened the trap door and silently shinned down into the brewery. It was a simple matter to climb back into the roof after I had dealt with King, detach the rope and return it to the bag. It had been my original intention to throttle the bugger face to face and enjoy the terror in his eyes but seeing the mallet I quietly picked it up and hit him with all the force I could muster. It was far too quick and painless. He should have suffered.

I stripped him to humiliate him further and so that all could see him for what he really was. Then it came to me. It was just like the old children's story and the Danny Kay film. Yes, King was now *'in the altogether'*. I emptied his pockets and dropped any cash or 'plastic' that I found into his brew. King thought he could buy anything with his money, buying off his affair with Alice by paying for her abortion. So much for his money now! In his office he had a stock of those Green Men masks he was selling. I took one and placed it back to front. Very apt, the two-faced bastard now really had two faces.

It was all done and dusted very efficiently within a quarter of an hour. I climbed back through the trap door, closed it behind me, and headed back the way I had come. Within half an hour of entering the garden, I had with military precision returned to my wheelchair and was mingling with the crowd. I felt an enormous wave of satisfaction wash over me.

Though initially doubtful, I had tried to convince myself that Bella King's action in providing Alice with the means of killing herself was unintended and done with the best of intentions to help her get a night's sleep. However, the sight of her in the television interviews as 'the grieving widow' totally changed my mind. She gloried in the notoriety that she had received indirectly due to Alice's suicide. Perhaps if she had been more honest about her involvement, I might have let her live. No one would give a young distraught girl a full bottle of sleeping tablets without thinking that these might be used to end her own life. Even if it was not deliberate, the mere wanton negligence of her action meant that she deserved to die.

I rode my bike along the river's edge, secreted it in the bushes near the pub and made my way to the rear. I had spent a week or two observing her actions following King's death and she always checked empty casks on the same night. Sure enough, there she was. I stepped out from behind the pile. I had only a few seconds to rejoice at the look of fear and amazement on her face before I shot her with a pistol I had acquired when in Helmand. They were ten a penny over there. I had originally smuggled it in as a souvenir. Personnel in wheelchairs are treated differently with regard to checks when entering the UK. It was over very quickly. I had previously written a note and I pinned this to her clothes. It took me an effort to drag her to the water's edge but once there, it was a comparatively easy matter to dispose of her body; or should have been.

She wore those tarty red shoes. I looked down and my anger boiled up within me. She was a woman of the world and she had been part of the reason for my sister (a naive, inexperienced young girl) lying in her grave. Stupidly, I grasped a shoe and like some schoolboy in a temper tantrum, intended to fling it as far as I could into the river. It slipped through my fingers and dropped into the reed bed. I spent precious moments searching for it but in the end, concluded it had sunk to the bottom. I dismissed this from my mind and concentrated upon the true matter in hand. After launching the corpse into the Severn, I returned to my motorbike and rode home.

After what I considered a justifiable killing of Bella King, all that was needed was to destroy The Green Man. I had come to regard this building as a place of evil where my lovely Alice had suffered. It had to be turned into rubble. Once more, my Army training and contacts throughout the country were put to good use. I had taken a training course in flying drones and obtaining plastic explosives is a relatively simple matter if you know where to shop. I incorporated extra pieces of electronic mechanisms in order more readily to direct the craft to its target. All worked well. The Green Man is no more.

Should my version of events ever reach the light of day, the reader will know that I am no longer alive and that I have joined Alice. I have tried to explain the reasons for my actions and my only deep regret is the necessity of having to murder a good and kind man to cover my deeds. Jim had come to the farm; I now know to tell me about our Bridgnorth appearance. It was one of those lax moments when I was out of my chair and in plain sight. He saw me and to my eternal shame, I killed him just for that. God forgive me.

Stan Till."

The officers looked at one another, each wrapped within his own thoughts. It had been a week now and a body had yet to be found.

Chapter 44

Bryn Edwards struggled to keep his footing as he made his way back up the railway embankment. After several mishaps involving him slipping back down and losing his spectacles, he at last arrived, red-faced and panting and sat down on the footbridge overlooking the track.

"Still fit as ever I see Bryn?"

"Oh, it's you is it Pitt? Not ready for my dissection table then yet?"

"No, sorry to disappoint you Bryn but I presently feel in rude health and why wouldn't I? Fresh Shropshire air, glorious sunshine and good company. What more could a man in the prime of life wish for?"

Bryn Edwards was still noisily sucking in air.

"Your super fit gym body counts for nought should you be hit by The Mallard travelling at one hundred and thirty miles an hour. You end up in pieces Ben, fit or not and it's not just posh folk like Anna Karenina who end their lives this way. You'd really have to not only be beyond reason but also pretty brave to jump from a railway bridge. Even so, I get at least a couple a year and I'll never get used to it. Why the hell didn't he take an overdose, slit his wrists or anything rather than this. I've got my minions bagging the pieces. It'll take a day or two. I'm afraid the Severn Valley Railway will be without a line until I'm finished and God knows when the poor driver will be in any fit state to return to work."

Edwards nodded across to a man huddled close to the track, clutching a silver emergency foil blanket around his shuddering torso.

"The passengers have been taken back to Bridgnorth in coaches but I've ordered an ambulance for that bloke. You just don't know how he'll react so I've persuaded him to spend the night in the hospital and notified his family of what's happening."

Pitt glanced down at the scene below. The engine was still belching steam and a small cloud of ashen smoke hung in the air. Here was a relic of a bygone age, a huge lumbering juggernaut like some mighty dinosaur cast out millions of years ago, only to be thrust forward into the Twenty-first Century. Men in white coverings and the local police in full uniform wandered along the track, heads down, eyes searching for any bloody piece of the jigsaw that was once a man.

"Can we be sure it was Till, Bryn?"

"Can't be sure of anything yet Ben. We are assuming it was male judging by the bits of clothing and sections of bone but the anatomical fleshy parts have so far eluded us. The clincher will be if we can find teeth or when your lads have taken the farm apart and perhaps found a toothbrush or hairbrush so that our DNA boys can get to work."

Pitt felt that he could not be sure until there was indeed proof. Here was a man who had managed to act out the role of a damaged veteran for many months, who had led him to believe that he had drowned in the Severn and who eventually had taken his own life in this gruesomely violent fashion. Though never confiding his views, Pitt had for once hoped that Till had indeed somehow cheated death and evaded the law. It would be several days before he would know the truth. Was this yet just another random suicide or was it indeed a man who had murdered three people?

Lightning Source UK Ltd.
Milton Keynes UK
UKHW010133060922
408385UK00001B/54

9 781803 693866